UNINTENTIONAL VICTIM

VICTIM

BOOK TWO

A MEL ADDISON MYSTERY

A NOVEL

BY

ANGELA ABDERHALDEN

Seventh Wave Books, LLC

Unintentional Victim
Book Two

Seventh Wave Books, LLC
2012

Seventh Wave Books, LLC
www.seventhwavebooks.com

First Paperback Edition: 2012

The characters, names, incidents, organizations, dialogue, and events portrayed in this book are fictitious. Any similarity to a real person, living or dead is coincidental and not intended by the author.

Unintentional Victim: a novel/ by Angela Abderhalden.

ISBN: 978-1-938852-02-2 (pbk)

Cover design by Jason Wilcox

Printed in the United States of America

ANGELA ABDERHALDEN

CHAPTER 1

I gasped, snapping the bag closed. It smelled like five day old vomit fermenting in the sun. It smelled like baby diapers marinated in fish guts. It smelled like a decomposing dead body. I opened the large, black garbage bag, released my breath to sniff again and flinched.

No, not a dead body. Rotten, putrefied, malodorous food. Opening my eyes, I hesitated before looking inside. *Yep, just food garbage.* I waggled my fingers encased in latex gloves. *Here goes nothing.* Suppressing a shudder, I reached inside and grabbed a handful.

Rancid goo slithered through my fingers. I shivered.

Ewee.

I snatched it again. The stinky slime squished in my palm. I tossed the mushy lump into the garbage can next to me. My whole body revolting at the feel and smell.

Yuck!

Reaching into the bag for the next smelly glob, I heard my brother's voice call from across the hall. "What is that horrendous odor?"

I smiled. *If I had to suffer, so did he.* "You wanted the garbage gone through."

"Oh man! That smells like..." He didn't finish his statement. Rich stuck his head in the conference room, a look of horror on his face.

I lifted the next piece of rot for him to see. The gunk slid down my fingers and plopped into the garbage can. My grin broadened at his scrunched-up, bad-beer face. *This piece smelled worse than the last.*

He shook his head, heading toward the front office. "I've got to open the door and get some air circulating in here. Man, that's putrid!"

With a chuckle, I tossed the next several handfuls into the garbage can. *Okay, I know I'm evil, but as long as Rich was suffering too, this couldn't be that bad.* Then I found some papers. These I placed on the plastic tablecloth protecting the conference table.

Dumpster diving is the least favorite activity I've done so far. However, what people throw away tells a lot about them and we needed all the help we could get.

I'm Melissa Addison and I work for Security Investigations in Quincy, Illinois. Rich is my oldest brother, an ex-cop, and John Huddleston is his partner, an ex-special forces Ranger. They run the only private investigator firm in my hometown. I'm a detective in training, so I get all the really fun jobs, like dumpster diving.

We're working on a criminal case for a defense lawyer. Two days ago, Simon Meddleson was arrested for murdering his sixty-nine year old mother. He, of course, claims he's innocent. Our job is to follow up on the cop's investigation and find a flaw, but the evidence is pretty convincing.

Last night, John discovered this trash bag at the Meddleson's neighbor. Only the neighbor's been gone for a week on a business trip. So, I got stuck sifting through the icky, gloppy mess.

I studied the papers, holding my hands out like a surgeon. One, an almost transparent piece, drew my attention. "Rich!"

"Yeah?"

I heard a fan turn on. "Come here. This is Meddleson's garbage." The hand-written, spidery scribbles lay crumbled on the table. I pushed it aside to see a telephone bill. Account name- Ruth Meddleson.

Rich hurried back. He soured his face glancing into the garbage can. "Phew. What?"

"Mrs. Meddleson's phone bill." I pointed with my gloved finger. I reached in for more papers.

Rich donned a pair of gloves. He looked it over then placed it even further from the mess. He picked up the crumbled paper and smoothed it out.

"Here... a shopping list, some junk mail, a receipt from a grocery story..." I looked at the next piece closely. "Looks like part of a letter and..." At the next handful, I screwed up my face. "Yucky. Snot rags." I tossed them on top of the goo.

Rich smiled as he read. "I wonder why this was at the neighbor's?" Although I knew it was a rhetorical question, I shrugged, tossing more disintegrating food away. "Don't forget to inventory that food," Rich said concentrating on the paperwork.

I paused mid-throw, staring at him. "You've got to be kidding." *Being siblings, he might be pulling my leg.*

Rich shook his head still not looking at me.

"I'm not going to-"

"You never know Mel, when something like that is important." Rich finally glanced up. "Seriously. Just keep a running list of what you're throwing out." He hesitated, his eyes panning to the can. "Or, what you think it might have been." His brotherly grin filled his entire face, spilling out of his eyes.

I stared.

"Really."

I snorted, snapping off the gloves. After retrieving pen and paper, I returned and gave Rich a disgusted look, which was lost on him. He was concentrating on the spidery handwriting. With another snort, I quickly listed what I thought I had thrown away. Some of it was *way* past prime.

Putting on a new pair of gloves, I continued my search. Near the bottom of the bag, I saw a pile of material. My brows knitted. Before my hand exited the bag, I whistled.

Rich's head snapped up.

I held up two faded, blue and yellow floral dish towels and a formerly white t-shirt. Both colored now in blood.

CHAPTER 2

Rich stared at the items then motioned not to lay them down. "Hold on. Let me get a paper bag. Vincent might want that tested." He quickly disappeared to return with a brown grocery bag.

I gently put the large white t-shirt splattered with still wet blood into the bag. The blue and yellow flowers on the hand towels were contrasted by the rusty brown streaks which colored them.

Rich closed the paper bag, taped it up, then wrote where the items had been located across the bag. Next he added that we both saw the contents and signed his name. He held out the pen for me to initial it.

I stripped off the glove and did as requested. Rich took the bag and went into his office. "Anything else in the bag, Mel?"

I expanded the now empty, smelly black bag. "Nope."

I could hear him asking for Vincent to call at his convenience. My eyes spied something white in the very bottom of the bag. It was tiny, hardly bigger then the tip of my pinky. I turned the garbage bag inside out to get it.

"What? Something else?"

"I don't know. What is this?" The matted clump perched on my finger as we both examined it. It looked sort of like a small owl pellet, only less dense. With hair. Very short hair. Short brown hair with a few whites ones interspersed. Hair glued together by blood. Matted, dried blood.

Once more Rich procured a paper bag and I shoved it in. We went through the same procedure with this one too.

"What do you think it was, Rich?"

A shrug greeted me as he left the conference room again. After returning he sat back down, grabbing the papers. "I don't know. If you're done with that," he said, pointing at the garbage. "Take it outside."

I stripped off the gloves, stuck them in before closing it up. Now I knew why Rich and John triple shredded all of their paperwork, everything, even the unimportant pieces.

I walked back in just as Pam, the secretary and receptionist, sat down at her desk from lunch. She scrunched up her face, fanning it with a file folder. "What a delicious smell you've found."

I chuckled. "John found it. I only unleashed it." As I passed Rich's office he motioned for me to wait.

After hanging up, he looked up. "Vincent wants us at the jail for a meeting with Simon this afternoon."

***

The jail meeting room was what one would expect, bleak and sterile. Gray walls. Beat-up, wood table. Standard issue, straight back, seen-better-days office chairs. Nothing else.

"Simon, this is Rich and Mel Addison from Security Investigations. They're helping with your case," Vincent Viking introduced us.

Simon was twenty-six. Dressed in the obligatory Adams County Jail jumpsuit. Thin and frail. He was clean shaven, but his shoulder length, greasy, stringy hair made him look creepy. In other words, just like I remembered him from when we were kids.

He was two years younger but I remembered him from my time hanging out with all of the public school kids. I went to Quincy Notre Dame, the private Catholic high school, but that didn't stop me from violating my parent's rules and hanging out with the 'less desirables' from the public school across town.

Simon shifted in his chair under Rich's critical, 'cop' eyes. "Hey, you arrested me once." Simon gave Viking a disbelieving look.

Viking nodded. "Rich is retired from the police force and is part owner of the investigative firm. I've hired them on your behalf to look into the police investigation."

"Good." Simon's grin grew to resemble the Cheshire cat's. "You can pick apart their case."

I glanced at my brother. His eyes showed that he was in 'cop mode'. Tense, yet relaxed. Relaxed, but vigilant. Vigilant and agitated. My attention swung back to the attorney as he opened his briefcase.

Viking pulled out a file. "Let's start with the bail hearing in two days. I'm pretty sure bail will be denied. Your record is not conducive to it." Viking continued as he flipped through the papers, "but we'll petition the court anyway."

Simon seemed to take that in stride. His eyes caught mine. A blank, almost uncaring look, then turned his attention back to his attorney.

"I want you to tell the detectives exactly what you told me. Run through the story again. They've seen my notes but I want them to hear it from you."

Simon rubbed his fingers together like a greedy person. "Where do ya want me to start?"

"The day of your mom's murder," Vincent answered.

"Okay." Simon took a breath. "I got up and did my usual routine."

Rich pulled out his ever-present notebook and looked at Viking. "Should I ask questions now or wait until the end?"

Viking shrugged with a look at Simon.

Simon merely motioned.

"What time did you get up?"

"Uh… Around ten or eleven, I guess. I really don't remember."

"Try to think of anything that might pinpoint when you woke up. It'll help us. Go on."

"Well, let's see. I grabbed a quick bite. Mom was just wakin' up. She yelled at me for gettin' in so late the night before. Guess I woke her up or somethin'."

"What time did you get in the night before?"

"I dunno. Two, three o'clock. It was late."

"Again, see if you can be more accurate," Rich said, his voice not yet dripping with frustration. "Did anyone see you?"

Simon looked down at the table. "Nope. The old people in the neighborhood are pretty much all in their houses or whatever by ten." His eyes flicked up to look at Rich then he stared at the table. "After I ate somethin' that morning, I took a shower. When I got out, Mom was arguing on the phone."

"With who?" Viking asked scribbling in his notes.

I glanced at Viking, apparently this was new information for him. *Was that irritation etching his face?*

"I dunno. I really didn't listen."

Viking let out his breath in frustration. "Simon, if we're going to help you, you need to tell us everything and remember as much as possible."

Simon's head was already bobbing. "Okay, let's see. She mentioned a name…" He seemed to be trying to see through the gray concrete wall. His fingers worrying the cuffs. "Okay, Bruce or Bryce maybe. She said something about that she couldn't do what he wanted, she was busy that night." He shrugged. "That's all I remember." He scratched his hand then placed his palms flat on the table.

"Do you know any Bruce or Bryce?" Rich asked.

"Nope." A finger twitched on his hand as his eyes rose to stare into Rich's blue, unreadable eyes. After several long, deadly quiet seconds, Simon jerked his hand to his chin and rubbed it then dropped his hands back to the table. "After she hung up…" Simon looked down at his hands, after a slight pause, he taped one finger then went on. "Well, let's see, she got another phone call as I walked out of the room. She said something like, 'This is not good' and something like 'I'll have to call and tell him'."

"Who was she talking to and talking about?" Viking asked before Rich could open his mouth.

"I dunno."

"Think, Simon."

The prisoner shook his head, rubbing his nose. "I dunno."

Viking sighed. "Okay, go on."

"I remember listening to some music for awhile. Sometime in the afternoon, I got up and ate lunch…" He squinted his eyes at the two men with a head cock. "No, I don't remember what time." He paused letting the sarcasm take affect. "Okay, I'll tell you that the soap opera Days of Our Lives was on. Mom watched it occasionally, wait no, she taped it. She was doing something with the check book or something at the time."

Rich made a note.

"I puttered around in my room for awhile. Mom yelled, asking if I'd go get her some soup from the store. She didn't feel good, an upset stomach. I told her that I was busy. We had a blow up. Then I gave in. I got a call on my cell right after I got home, from Punky in St. Louis. I was going to meet him at the club down there. We made plans and I took another shower and got dressed. I asked Mom for some money. We had another big blow up over that, as usual. She's always stingy with the money. I left after she finally gave me a twenty for gas. I left."

"What time? Have you thought about it, Simon?" Viking asked.

"I have, but I still can't be sure when I left. I was really mad at Mom. I dunno. The news was on the rock station I listen to, if that helps."

Viking took a deep breath. "Go on."

"I drove down to St. Louis. I met Punky at Rascals, a dance club there. We hung out until it closed, at three." Simon scratched his hand again then rubbed his nose. "I drove Punky to his apartment and crashed at his place. We woke up late, around noon or something 'cause his girl was heading out to eat. I just hung at Punky's for the day. We were planning on doing the club thing again. Chrissy, Punky's girlfriend, was gonna get me a date with a new girl at her work." Simon grinned at us. "I never pass up a free date, she was paying. We did the club thing for awhile. The girl was a loser-"

"Her name?" Rich interrupted.

"Uh, I dunno… Denna or Diane or something like that. I was kinda high at the time." Simon sniffed and looked at Viking. "I can tell'em right? I mean, he works for us, right?"

Viking nodded.

"I was really high. Punky had scored some really good stuff earlier and I wasn't on the job, so I could do it with him, ya know."

"On the job?" Rich asked.

Simon looked at Viking.

"Tell him," Viking said.

"I steal cars. We get a request in, the boss gives it to us, me and Punky. We find a matching car. Steal it and take it to the shop in East St. Louis."

9

Rich nodded in understanding.

"Anyway, I hadda fight with Punky and I headed home here. I mean, if I'm gonna fight with someone, it might as well be Mom. At least I've got my own room here. Anyway, I get back in town and this cop pulls me over. I barely stop and three other cars are around me. They pulled me out of the car and arrested me for Mom's murder." Simon looked down at the table, sniffed once then looked up at us. "I ain't killed my mom. I love her."

I could tell that no matter what else happened, Simon was at least being honest about that.

"The police have witnesses that place you at your home the night your mom was killed," Rich said. "What do you say about that?"

Simon shook his head. "I dunno. I was down in St. Louis or at least on my way there. When I left, Mom was sitting in her lounge chair eating and smoking. Winnie was lounging on her lap. He was licking her bowl."

"Winnie?" I spoke for the first time.

"Winston. Mom's dog. Winnie for short. A Shih Tzu."

I looked at the others but they were busy writing on their papers. I shrugged at the information as Viking began speaking.

"Okay. Can anyone besides Punky verify your whereabouts?"

"Uh, Chrissy and that other one, Diane or Denna or whoever. Lots of people were in the club, but I don't remember anyone by name." Simon rubbed his ear lob.

"What's Punky's real name?" Rich asked.

"I dunno."

"Excuse me?" Rich asked him with an incredulous tone. "You did drugs with him, worked with him, partied with him and you don't even know his name?"

Simon shook his head. "Just Punky. I think Chrissy called him Jeff once, maybe."

Rich continued to stare at Simon for a minute. "What about Chrissy?"

Simon shook his head. "Just Chrissy."

"Where does she live?"

"I dunno. I've only seen her at Punky's or the club."

Rich actually sighed. "Okay, where does this Punky live?"

"I dunno the exact address."

This time Viking sighed, again. "Simon, we need to verify your whereabouts so we can break open the police case against you. We can't do that if you aren't going to help us."

"I really don't remember the address," Simon said, lowering his head a little. "I, uh, I can give you directions."

Rich flipped his notebook to a clean page and put the pad and pen near Simon's hands. "Write them down."

Simon took the pen and diligently wrote for some time, stopping occasionally to look off in the distance as if trying to remember where he had gone.

Rich turned to me and rolled his eyes. I almost smiled at him. Simon was not making our job any easier.

Shortly, we finished up. Simon was escorted out of the room first, then we left. Viking shook his head at Rich when we were near his car.

"I know, Rich," Viking said with a grin. "I know. Just do your best. Keep me up to date with what you find out. We'll have another meeting before the first hearing."

"Did you want to get the towels and shirt tested?"

"Let me think on it over night. We couldn't have the results back by the first hearing anyway. I'll let you know tomorrow."

We waved as he pulled away. The jail wasn't far from the office. I turned to Rich as we walked. "What do you think?"

Rich shook his head. "I just hope that Tom didn't screw up the investigation."

"So, you think Simon did it?"

Rich shrugged. "I won't get the police file until tomorrow, after Viking gets it. We'll see."

"Simon lied," I said after a couple of seconds of silence.

"Yeah. He was doing something else in St. Louis, if he was even there."

I agreed with Rich. Simon either wasn't telling us something or had left a big chunk of time unaccounted for on purpose. "Where do we go from here?"

Rich opened the door to the office and held it for me. "Let me talk to John. He has a lot of contacts in the St. Louis area. He's going to head back down there to track Simon's whereabouts. I think tomorrow you should re-canvas the neighborhood."

CHAPTER 3

Another door slammed in my face. I stared at it for half a second before sighing. This was the last house and not one of the people had been nice. Not one. So odd for this town. Usually people were talkative, often to the point of not being able to shut them up. I backed off from the doorway to look around the neighborhood again.

The single story houses were all middle class in fairly decent shape. A few were becoming run down but for the most part they were well maintained; all seemed to have been built in the mid to late seventies.

As I sat on the concrete steps near the street, contemplating what to do next, I rubbed my feet in my tennis shoes trying to massage them. My thoughts returned to the neighborhood that I was in.

None of the neighbors seemed to want Simon back in the area. Not that I blamed them. From childhood on, Simon was forever in trouble. From minor vandalism to disruptive behavior in elementary school. From joy riding to 'inciting racial unrest' in middle school. From car theft to suspected drug sales in high school.

The aching in my foot eased just a little. With another glance around, I took a deep breath. I felt like a door to door salesman trying to pawn off bad vacuum cleaners on them or a telemarketer calling at supper. I wondered if John had any better luck in St. Louis. Or Rich with the police reports.

Rich! My oldest, biggest pain in the butt brother as far as today went. The other day going through the garbage and today getting doors slammed in my face. *I didn't need this aggravation. And my feet hurt! Why did I let myself get dragged into this?*

I had taken the job two months ago as a favor to him because his secretary had gone on maternity leave. I was to answer phones and do computer work until Pam could return. I agreed because I was a recent return to Quincy myself. I had lost a husband and son in a car accident earlier in the year. Returning to Quincy, home, felt right.

What I hadn't needed was having a gun shoved in my face the first day on the job. That had lead to four people dying, me finding one of the bodies, along with Rich and myself getting beaten up. Rich has just gotten his arm out of his cast.

In the end, the killers were found, almost resulting in my own death, and the case solved. But John and Rich had offered me a job with them because I was so good at being nosy. John's words were 'You're a natural'. I had accepted the job in a brief moment of insanity.

I know, I'm crazy . But there it is and here I am walking my tennis shoes bare to help a loser like Simon try to stay out of prison for the rest of his life. Personally, I couldn't care less if he rotted in there forever.

My cell phone interrupted my thoughts. I checked the caller ID before answering it. It was Mitch, my other brother, also older than me and a cop.

"Hey, sorry I missed your call."

"Yeah. You haven't answered it in a couple of days. I thought you were ditching my calls." I chuckled, knowing it wasn't the case but I loved teasing him when I could.

"Sorry, been busy."

"So I heard. Tina. How's it going, Casanova?"

"Fine."

I could almost hear the blush in his voice, a hard thing to do. "Getting kind of serious with this one?"

"Nothing like that."

With the irritation in his voice, I knew I was getting close to the truth. My grin got wider.

"Look, what did you want?"

"Testy."

He sighed. "What? I'm kind of busy."

"Uh huh. I just wanted some information on Simon Meddleson, but I found out the harder way."

"Yeah."

"Okay from the tone in your voice… Let me guess, you're unhappy that Rich and I are looking into this."

"Mel, you know as well as I do that Simon is scum. Like me, half the guys here have arrested him, not that many of the charges stuck. Slicker than dog snot."

"Yeah, I remember him from high school, but he *is* innocent until proven guilty."

Another sigh from the phone. "Did you have anything specific in mind? And you know I can't talk about the case."

"I know. And I don't need your help now. Thanks, *Big Brother*."

"Yeah. Speaking of that-"

"Don't change the subject."

Mitch chuckled. We had always been close, being only fourteen months apart. Out of all of my siblings, I felt closest to him. "How are you doing? I haven't asked in awhile."

My heart twisted. My gut clenched. I swallowed back the hurt and tears. It was only eight months since I had lost my husband and only child in a car accident. And I still wasn't used to this question, especially coming out of the blue like this. "Time is healing, I guess."

He huffed.

I could never put much by him.

"Sure. If you want to talk-"

"Then let's talk about Tina." I interrupted him, relieved that he wasn't following up on his line of thought.

"Man, you are irritating. Later."

I chuckled as I closed the phone. Yes, I was getting really good at dodging the family's questions about 'how I was doing'. With a sigh, I rubbed my feet again. *Back to canvassing the neighborhood.*

I looked down the street and noticed an older man walking his dog. I frowned, knowing he didn't live in the neighborhood. I watched as the dog did his business.

He was a cute little dog, maybe a toy poodle, and he looked old even from this distance. I smiled, thinking that people and their dogs begin to look alike as they grow older.

Surprisingly, the man reached down and, with a plastic bag, retrieved the dog doo. I knew the city had an ordinance about dog poop, but I had never actually seen anyone do it. Or the cops enforce it for that matter.

He nodded as he got close. "Nice afternoon. Not too hot."

I smiled back, wondering where he lived and if he walked his dog in this neighborhood all the time. "Yeah, but I hear before Halloween it is supposed to get cold. Still, the weather seems to be sticking on the nicer side." I paused as he let his dog pee in the grass. "Do you live around here?"

He studied me.

I kept smiling at him to show him that it was an innocent question. His gray, owl-like eyebrows furrowed in thought. He was in pretty good shape for being in his seventies, I guessed. His hazel eyes were still sharp, if nothing else.

"I live about four blocks away. Why do you ask?"

I stood up and handed him a generic business card. I wasn't allowed my own yet. "I work for Security Investigations. We're looking into the Meddleson murder for the defendant's attorney."

A smile greeted me showing a mouth full of healthy teeth. As I finished my sentence, he chuckled. "So I heard. Mrs. Beaverton…" He pointed down the street to a faded yellow house. "Told me that a young lady was canvassing the neighborhood trying to get Simon out of jail."

"Actually, I think the fink should stay in jail whether he did it or not, but that's not how the system works. He's allowed his day in court. If he did it, I hope they give him the death penalty, but until that point, he's innocent until proven guilty."

The older man's smile increased. "Good speech. Has it worked on any of the neighbors?"

I chuckled. "Not one."

"It doesn't surprise me."

"Actually me either, but I have to try." I shrugged at him, figuring he wouldn't talk to me either.

"Simon wasn't a bad kid, just mixed up. He needed more structure in his life." The older man shook his head. "That's the problem with you kids these days, no one takes responsibility for their actions anymore. Parents don't make their kids do anything. No discipline."

I smiled. I was twenty-nine, hardly a 'kid'. "How well did you know Simon?"

"What's your name?" he asked, looking at the business card I had handed him.

"Melissa Addison. I only work for the agency. I'm not a private investigator."

"Just a peon?"

"That's me." He was more like what I had expected in the neighborhood.

"Look, I really shouldn't be seen talking to you. The neighbors are all friends of mine. Come talk to me later on tonight. I live on Lind Street, just four blocks over. White house with green trim, you can't miss it." He stuck the card in his pocket and started walking away.

"Okay, I will. Sir?" I waited until he turned then asked the question I should have asked right away, "What's your name, sir?"

"Sir?" He pulled his dog's leash to stop its forward motion. "At least you're polite. I like that. Earl Boden."

"Thank you, Mr. Boden."

Earl tugged at his dog. "Come on, Scruffy."

***

"Mel, is that you?" Rich's voice floated down the hallway of the detective agency as I entered the building.

I smiled at Pam who merely looked up at me. "Yeah, Rich. Coming Bossman." I headed down the hall to his office.

Security Investigations is located in downtown Quincy, Illinois. We inhabit one of the older buildings there. When I had left town those many years ago, the downtown had fallen into disuse. Everyone was building and moving out near the mall and other areas. Then about ten years ago, there was a resurgence of renewal in the downtown area and it was rebuilt becoming a growing business area again.

Quincy is on the upswing in its growth too. We're kind of stuck in the middle of no where, on the 'belly' of Illinois, with the Mississippi separating us from Missouri and Iowa. Geographically between Chicago and St. Louis, we're in the middle of territorial disputes between the various criminal fractions inhabiting those cities. Being the biggest city in the surrounding area at around 45,000 people, you'd think that we would be well known. Fifteen miles down the Mississippi is Hannibal, Missouri. Smaller, but better known, thanks to Mark Twain.

We have the usual share of small city problems, but the biggest problem is boredom. Of course, the police have been serving more federal arrest warrants then ever due to the drug and gang fractions discovering the Quincy is a great little city off the beaten path. A great place to vacation. Go figure. Quincy, a vacation spot for criminals.

I stopped at the door to Rich's office to see him deep in paperwork.

Rich lifted his head. "Anything with the neighbors?"

"Nada, but, I ran into an older guy walking his dog. He might provide some background on Simon. Mr. Boden lives four blocks away, so I doubt he'll be able to help with the actual murder." I sighed. "And so far he's the only one to give me the time of day."

Rich frowned.

"How about you?" I leaned on the doorpost with my hands in my pockets.

"Uncooperative," Rich said. "But I really didn't expect anything else." He shook his head. "Even Mitch seems upset."

"Yeah, with me too. He's getting crabby in his old age." I smiled at Rich, who smirked back. I loved to tease both of them about being older then me. I was the second youngest in the family. The list went Rich, Teresa, Mitch, me, then the real baby, Cameron. "Besides, knowing Simon due to the 'job', he's got other things on his mind."

"Oh, yeah? What?"

"Tina."

Rich chuckled. "Should have figured it was a woman. You're all alike. Trying to hook a man…" He drifted off.

I chuckled. "Mitch arrested Simon but I take it the charges were dropped?"

"Yeah. I arrested him too. I caught him joy riding with some other kids. Got off with a slap on the wrist." Rich's eyes slightly narrowed. "Even if he didn't kill his Mom, he's done enough stuff to warrant prison anyway."

Silence hung in the air for a few seconds. "Unfortunately," Rich said, picking up some papers. "That's not how the system works."

"Yeah," I replied. "Now that you've read the police report, do you think he did it?"

Rich didn't answer right away. "Anything I say comes out wrong." He paused. His blue eyes catching mine. "Tom's a good cop. I know how he works. I can't believe he cut any corners or messed up the investigation. If he thinks he has enough evidence to convict Simon of the crime, then you can pretty much make book on it."

I nodded in agreement with my brother, but there were a few disturbing loose ends not accounted for in the police investigation. Obviously the cops and the District Attorney felt they had enough for a conviction.

I looked down at my shoes. When I looked back up, Rich was leaning back in his chair staring at a point over my right shoulder. "What did Tom say?"

"I know better than to ask him, he won't talk to me about it. Rightfully so. I just hope he didn't screw up. I don't want this to come between us."

"Have you heard from John today?"

Rich nodded his head moving back to his paperwork. "So far, Meddleson's story is not holding any water. John called this morning from St. Louis. He's supposed to check with a couple of other people then be back tonight."

"After I talk with Mr. Boden tonight, what do you want me to do? Anything else to look into in the Meddleson case?"

"Did you ever finish running all the names through the data bases?"

"Not yet. I was going to finish that this afternoon." I glanced at my watch. It was already four-thirty.

"Sounds good."

"Okay." I turned to leave then looked back at Rich. "Did that accountant figure out the bank mess yet?" The agency had a forensic accountant that could rebuild Mrs. Meddleson's financial picture from the information recovered by the lawyer. Starting with checking account information and such, he could figure out where all her money was and where it went, but it took some time.

"Not yet."

Pam's voice drifted down the hall that Rich had a phone call, a possible new client.

I headed to my office as Rich picked up his phone. My 'office' was really a misnomer. After I started working for the guys, they converted one of the conference rooms into my 'office'. I still didn't have a real desk. I only had one small file drawer. So my stuff was spread out on the big table.

I turned on the computer. It never took long to run the data bases for names but it was tedious work. And since I was the trainee here, I got stuck doing the grunt work. As the computer booted up, I headed to the front office to grab a soda from the fridge.

I had no more than sat down when Rich called for me. With a glance at the list of waiting names, I headed to see what he wanted. "Yeah?"

He hung up the phone, still scribbling notes on a piece of paper. He finished writing before he looked up. "I've got a possible new client coming in to talk to me in about an hour."

I glanced at my watch.

"I want you to stay for the meeting. If we take her on, I'll turn her over to you."

"And this lady's problem?"

Rich shrugged. "She wasn't real specific over the phone. Something about she just moved here and wants us to do some background on a former boyfriend. Sounds like mostly computer work and besides being a woman…"

Oh great, more computer work. "Sure."

"Actually, she specifically asked if we had a woman detective she could talk to. I was getting the impression that she doesn't like or trust men. So, if we take her, she'd probably feel more comfortable with you anyway."

"Hmmm."

"And don't mention right away that I used to be a cop, okay?"

"Why?"

"She said she didn't trust the cops. They were no help at all."

CHAPTER 4

Rich tapped on my door frame as he passed with a lady following him. I stood up and headed to the next room. This was still a conference room. Rich motioned for the lady to sit in a chair and waited until she did before sitting himself. I took the seat next to Rich.

She was an ordinary looking lady, nothing very outstanding about her at all. Her brown hair framed her face and if she was smiling she probably would be pretty. She wore jeans and a flannel top over a T-shirt. No jewelry to speak of and almost no make-up. She appeared slightly nervous as she glanced at me.

I smiled.

"I'm Rich Addison. This is Melissa Addison, my sister."

"Call me Mel," I added quickly, holding out my hand.

She shook Rich's first, then mine. "I'm Romania Trolowski. Call me Roma." She gave me a slight smile. "Do you own the place with your brother?"

"No. John Huddleston runs it with Rich. I'm merely a goffer." I could tell that Rich was letting me make her feel comfortable. And I also saw the quick warning glance that he gave me. It helped out a lot that we were siblings, non-verbals worked great.

"I uh, I uh…" Roma cleared her throat. "I really wanted to work with a female detective."

"I'm not licensed yet, still in training, but Rich has a good number of years doing things like this. John has too. We treat every client the same, whether it's a big case or a small one. We all give it one hundred percent."

Roma looked at Rich. "How long have you been in this business?"

"Formally two years. Before that, I did other investigations for various clients for over fifteen." Rich paused. "Why don't you tell us the reason you came here and we'll see if we can help you?"

Roma glanced at me again then nodded. She looked down at her hands before looking back up at us. "You'll probably think I'm a nut case. All the cops do. I can't get them to help me, anywhere I go. This is my last move. I refuse to be chased again. I'm getting real tired of this."

Rich frowned. "Start at the beginning, Roma. Why specifically do you want to hire us?"

She reached into her purse and pulled out a picture of a man. She handed it to Rich, who flashed it to me, then laid it on the table in front of him. Nothing special about him. Black short hair. Almost nerdy looking. Your average guy.

"He's been chasing me for about ten years. We dated for about a month. He refuses to believe that I don't want to date him, no matter what I've tried. What I need from you is to find him for me. He's scheduled to be paroled soon. Just find him and make sure… well, I don't know. Just make sure he stays in Texas, I guess."

Rich waited until Roma looked at him. "He's stalking you, isn't he?"

"Yeah," she said. "I feel that I don't have a life anymore. I'm still looking over my shoulder everywhere I go."

"Have you tried contacting the correctional facility in Texas where he's incarcerated?" Rich asked.

"No. Well, I haven't gotten internet yet. And I lost their number." She blushed. "To be honest with you, I can't work up the nerve to call. I know once he's out, he'll find me. I guarantee it. I just…" She hung her head. "I… I'm scared."

"And if he is out?"

"I don't know. I just want to know where he is. Can you do that?"

"We can," Rich said. "Let me explain about our fees. If you agree, I'll have you sign a contract with us. We'll need a fee up front. You'll get regular updates on your case and any extra expenses beyond what we discuss tonight will be approved by you on a case by case basis." Rich pulled out the standard contract and began to explain it.

After she signed it and gave Rich a check, he asked me to get her a soda before we started getting more of the facts. When I returned, she appeared more relaxed and trusting.

"Tell us about this stalker. Start ten years ago so we have the full story," Rich said as he picked up his pen.

Roma looked at me as I also grabbed a pen to take notes. "Well, we used to work together, Devon and me. Oh, that's his name by the way. Devon Miles."

"Where did you work?" I glanced at Rich who gave me a slight head nod for me to take over the conversation.

"California. I moved out to San Diego after I graduated high school. I originally intended on Los Angeles to be an actress but I got hired by a firm,

Sethdran Processing to do data entry and it paid really well. My acting career got put on hold and just never got off the ground. I don't really regret that. Anyway, he was really a nice guy. Or so I thought. He hung around my crowd, you know kind of on the fringes. I really didn't want to date him but well he seemed kind of sad and all, so I did. The first date was okay. So I went out with him on another. It just kind of developed into a thing that gave me something to do on the weekends. I wasn't serious and told him that many times. He didn't seem to be put off." Roma took a long drink of her soda.

"We dated for about a month or so. Finally, he just started getting on my nerves. You know, always wanting to know where I was and stuff. So I just called it off. At first, he stopped calling and all. He would still talk to me at work all the time, but..." She twirled the can in her hands. "It was around this time that I started noticing little things that were happening. This is where it starts getting weird. I would feel like I was being followed, but I couldn't really see anyone. My mail was...well, there would be days when I wouldn't get mail then a couple of days later, I'd get a whole stack of it. I talked to the mailman one day about it. He assured me that he delivered mail to my box almost everyday. Then I began to actually listen to Devon talking to me at work. He would make a comment occasionally about something I had done the night before. Stuff he shouldn't have known."

"Did you go to the police in San Diego?" Rich asked still scribbling notes.

"Not at first. I didn't know what he was doing at the time. Looking back on it, I should have, but I just didn't know at the time."

Rich motioned for her to go on.

"Things began to escalate after that. And I started seeing him all the time. Almost every place I went, I saw him. I sort of blew up at him about it." Roma nodded at Rich as he went to open his mouth. "I know now that was the wrong thing to do. I've since gotten a lot smarter, but at the time I didn't know. All he wanted me to do was to go out with him again. I refused and told him to leave me alone. As you can expect, it did no good. He started leaving notes at my desk at the office and in my car. I spoke to my supervisor at work. It did no good. It kept getting worse. I couldn't go anywhere without him being there. Then, for awhile, it seemed to stop. I'm not sure why to be honest with you. I thought my problems were over but I was wrong."

"What was the longest he left you alone and did you ever figure out why?"

"About two months and no, I never did. He got fired during that time. My bosses wouldn't tell me why they fired him." Roma took another drink then played with the can a little. "I started to live again. I met another guy, Trent, and we dated. Devon didn't like it. He began again. Devon busted out Trent's apartment windows, his car windows and dented up Trent's car horribly. The police couldn't do much, they told me. No proof it was Devon. Trent and I broke up, of course. I guess that was Devon's intention. He sent me presents and letters, again. I moved to a new place. A week later I got my first present there. It was scary. Finally, I could take no more. I applied and took a demotion in Sethran in Texas. I didn't think he'd follow me. I was wrong. A month later it started over. He called day and night, for hours on end." Roma was staring at the table as she spoke and now sat motionless, obviously reliving the incidents.

Rich glanced at me and tilted his head.

I gave him a quick nod. "Roma, why did Devon go to prison?"

"Oh." Roma blushed slightly, bringing herself mentally back into the room. "Sorry. He threatened me. Again the cops weren't much help. I got a restraining order, which seemed to anger him even more. Of course, he totally ignored it. One night he was following me. I was mad because, well, because I had no life. I went through a yellow light, well, it was sort of orange, if you get my meaning."

I smiled. *It's not like I hadn't done that before.*

"He tried to follow and caused an accident. I stopped at a nearby gas station and told the police I was a witness to the accident and told them about the restraining order. They took my statement and put him in jail for about four days. Two days after he got out my car was fire-bombed. Three days after that, he broke into my apartment. I was meeting with a police officer at the apartment that day. The cop caught him red-handed. When he was in court, he said some nasty things to and about the judge." She chuckled. "That made the judge mad. He sentenced Devon to two years in prison. It's coming up on one year now. I moved to Florida, then here a week ago."

"Who knows that you moved here?"

"The only people who know are my parents. They won't give out that information to anyone, even old friends. They know what I've gone through."

"How did you come to pick Quincy?" I asked leaning back in my chair, glancing at Rich. He was still scribbling notes.

"I threw a dart at a map of the country. My parents live in Oregon, by the way. I wanted to be in the mid-west somewhere. The dart hit Illinois. Then I took out a map of Illinois and closed my eyes and pointed. Quincy's where my finger landed."

"Here's what we'll do, Roma," Rich began, "first thing in the morning, Mel'll get on the horn to see if Devon is still incarcerated. She'll call you immediately with that information. Then we'll go from there. If he's still in prison and you decide to stop at that, we'll reimburse you your money, minus Mel's time. If he's out or anything else, we'll sit down and decide what to do. Okay?"

Roma blinked several times, almost as though she was trying not to cry. "I appreciate you taking this seriously. I usually don't get much understanding from people, since I can't ever really prove that Devon is behind all of this..."

"I used to be a cop, Roma," Rich said with a gentle look in his eye. He reached out and patted her hand. "I've worked a stalking case before. I

22

understand the terror it causes and the fear you've had to live with. When we sit down to discuss this, I'll have gotten the full story on the laws so we'll know just where we stand here." Rich paused. "I'll tell you one thing, since you moved across state lines, now if he continues to terrorize you, he can be prosecuted under Federal Law, that carries a much heftier sentence."

Roma looked relieved. "I feel better already."

Rich smiled as we stood up. She shook both of our hands with a happier look in her eye and a smile on her face. Her walk was lighter than when she had come in as I led her to the front. A confident ring to her 'thanks again' as we parted made me smile. I returned to find Rich in his office. "Anything else, Rich? I need to head over to Mr. Boden's to talk to him about Simon."

"No. Thanks for staying, Mel. Just do the computer check on the stalker first thing in the morning."

"Can we actually help her?"

"It depends on a lot of things." Rich shook his head with a frown. "Stalkers. Bad business."

***

Earl Boden's house was a small two-story, white with green trim bungalow. It had a big front porch with a huge swing, and I could tell that he took pride in his lawn. Flowers were still blooming in the beds and in hanging planters on his porch. The lawn was manicured to look better than many golf greens.

I knocked on the door. In the background, I could hear soft music drifting out of the open window, big band music. Tommy Dorsey, if I wasn't mistaken. He was a favorite of my Mom's so I'd heard his music a lot growing up.

The little dog that I had seen him walking barked at me through the screen door. I smiled as Boden approached through the living room. "Hi, Mr. Boden. You said that you'd talk to me about Simon Meddleson. I'm Melissa Addison."

Earl Boden motioned me in. "I'm repotting some plants in the sun room. We can talk back there while I work, if you don't mind. Scruffy, it's okay boy." Boden turned to me. "He's very protective."

"I see that." I smiled down at the now growling dog. The white toy poodle couldn't have been over six pounds with rocks tied to his paws but he tried to sound tough. I followed Boden through his house.

The inside of the house was just as meticulous as the outside. Everything was immaculately clean. It reminded me of Mom's house. We always have kidded her about her cleanliness, saying that it was cleaner eating off her floors than most people's kitchen tables. As I headed through his kitchen, I had visions that even the germs were lined up and cleaned on a regular basis.

Boden was talking over his shoulder. "I'm almost finished. Scruffy, quiet. Would you like something to drink, Ms. Addison?"

"Uh, no thank you, Mr. Boden. And call me Mel."

Earl turned to me. "Okay, Mel. What do you want to know about Simon?" He motioned me to take a seat on one of his chairs perched around a small table where he was working. The sun room was more of an enclosed porch. It was screened with a ceiling fan twirling away. *Nice with today's weather.* The openness of it made you feel like you were outside, yet it was as spotless as the rest of his house. Even the dirt that he was using to repot the plants seemed clean. Scruffy laid down near the wall watching me, but content to stay quiet for now.

"Well, as you know, Simon's accused of killing his Mom."

Boden nodded his head with a sad look on his face. He reached into the big bag of dirt and scooped some out to put into a smaller pot.

"He claims that he didn't kill her. We've been hired by his attorney to re-interview witnesses and such to substantiate his story." I paused watching the old man work. It seemed to me that not a speck of dirt fell anywhere except where he wanted it to go, as though an unseen force field kept the dirt in place. I shook myself to get back to the subject at hand and continued, "I was sent to talk with the neighbors about the night Mrs. Meddleson was killed, to see if they heard anything or such."

Boden glanced up from his pot. "The police already did that. They came up with nothing."

"Yes, but Vincent Viking has us retracing the police steps looking for anything they missed."

"Did anyone hear anything? Did the police do something wrong?" Earl asked pausing in his work, hands held over the new pot with a plant.

"No one will talk with me. None of the neighbors will even confirm to me that they were home. I haven't gotten any more information than the police did, actually less."

Boden nodded, relieved. "Doesn't surprise me. All the neighbors were really upset when Simon came back to town." He made a gurgle noise in his throat. "Good. No one wants him back."

"That was the impression I was getting."

He went back to work on his plant. "What do you want with me? I don't live near enough to have heard or seen anything."

"I was hoping that you could give me a little background on Simon and his Mom. You said that you were friends with everyone in the neighborhood."

Earl paused again. "I don't want Simon out either, young lady." His bushy eyebrows narrowed making his face seem even more like an owl's. His eyes dark and beady.

"I understand that. Could you just give me a feel for his home life?"

Boden didn't speak for a few minutes while he went back to work. He seemed to be doing a great deal of thinking about whether to help me or not. I waited patiently, figuring it would be a waste of my time anyway.

"I suppose it wouldn't hurt to answer some of your questions, I guess," Earl said finally, his face relaxing as he spoke. "Ruth was a good woman, she deserved better than Simon as a son. Most of the neighbors thought she was sort of stuck up, but it was just that she was unsure of herself, I think."

"Do you mind if I take notes?" Some people didn't like it when you wrote down what they said.

"No, go ahead."

"I know from the information that his attorney has given us that Simon's dad died when he was little. Do you know what from?"

"It was an industrial accident at the old fertilizer plant. Gone now, of course. There was an explosion. He died. Simon was, oh, maybe two or three."

I nodded as I scribbled the information. I knew all of this, I was just breaking ground with easy questions. Something Rich taught me. It eases people into answering some harder questions. "Were they already living at the house here in the neighborhood?"

"No. They moved here shortly thereafter. I think Ruth used some of the insurance money to buy the house. She has always owned it free and clear." Boden set one plant to the side and started on the next one.

"You said that Simon was mixed up. What did you mean by that?"

Earl paused in scooping out more dirt. "Ruth did the best she could but without a man in the house. Simon got away with a lot of things. At first, Ruth could control him, until maybe he was twelve. After that, he pretty much did what he wanted." He tapped the dirt down and added more.

"This was after he was sent to reform school, right?"

"Yes. He was forever in trouble, as I'm sure you already know." Earl shook his head. "That boy would try anything he could think of, just to see if he could get away with it. And he usually did." There was a defeated tone in his voice or maybe skepticism.

"Do you know of any of Simon's friends?"

"Well, I know he used to hang out with that Douglas boy. The one that got caught in Springfield in that bank robbery, but that was a long time ago. After he got into high school, I don't think he hung out around home much. I know for a fact it upset Ruth, but by this time, Simon ran the house. I think Ruth basically gave up on him."

"Was he doing anything illegal that you know of?"

"You mean recently, when he killed Ruth?"

"Yeah. I understand that he might have started selling drugs in high school, then he disappeared after graduation. Do you know what he was doing during those years?"

Boden shrugged. "Can't say for sure. Ruth told me once that he had gotten involved with some nasty people in St. Louis, but I didn't care enough to really ask, to be honest with you."

"Why did he come back to live with his mom?"

"I wouldn't call it living with her. More like sponging off her again. He got in a bind money-wise, from what I heard. He needed money again. Only this time Ruth refused to give him much, is my understanding." Boden's face showed his disgust.

"Hmmm," I commented, writing up the information.

"I heard he got it anyway."

"Got what?" I looked up to see Boden staring at me. His hazel eyes boring into mine.

"Ruth's money. One of the neighbors told me that he cleaned out her strong box where she kept her money, six hundred dollars worth, and took her credit cards." Boden's hands were resting on the side of the large bucket of dirt. They were strong looking hands, as though he worked a lot with his hands.

"So I heard too. At least some of it," I said with a nod. "So, do you think he did it?"

"It wouldn't surprise me at all." Boden's eyes flicked to the plants on the table. The last pot sitting on the table was waiting for him.

"You've lived in the neighborhood the whole time?"

"Yes. My wife and I moved here a couple of years before Ruth. Most of the block is still the old neighborhood. Some younger couples have moved in around the area, but there're still a lot of us old fogies."

"How well do you know Ruth's neighbors?"

Boden smiled. "Back in the old days, we used to have quite a Bridge tournament most weekends. After my wife died, well.... Then it was just Mrs. Beaverton, Mrs. Hamilton, and Mr. and Mrs. Allen that played. Now, well, we don't play much anymore."

"Did Ruth play?"

"Not Bridge. I used to play Canasta with her and Mrs. Beaverton, occasionally Mrs. Hamilton. This was mostly after Simon left town." The smile on his face showed that they must have enjoyed the cards. He finished with the last pot and began putting things away and cleaning up after himself.

"Do you know if any of the neighbors heard anything the night Mrs. Meddleson died?"

Boden shook his head. "Mr. and Mrs. Allen on the one side of Ruth are hard of hearing, so they couldn't have heard anything. Bill Timmerman on the other side was out of town that night, still is. He travels a lot. Whenever he leaves, he always asks me to watch his place and collect his newspapers. It's easier than asking the paperboy to hold deliveries. That youngster can't remember much of anything. In my day, we took pride in doing a job right. Now a days, they just want money for little or no work."

"Do you take your dog for a walk every night in the neighborhood?" I looked down at the little, cute 'mutt' sleeping. He seemed almost as old as Mr.

Boden. Scruffy opened his eyes and lifted his head as though he understood English. As his master went back to talking, he yawned and laid his head down on his paws.

"Usually in the mornings. On nice days, I sometimes walk in the afternoon too, like today. I like to be inside before dark these days. Too many criminals out there taking advantage of old people."

"Did you hear or see anything on either of the days you walked your dog?"

Boden put the bag of potting soil in a large bucket, then he placed it in a cabinet before really thinking about my question. As he thought, he wiped the table down. "Not really." He grabbed a broom nearby to sweep the floor.

I looked down. I didn't see any dirt there. Since I had been watching him, not one grain of dirt had fallen off the table; the force field had worked properly. Yet he was diligently sweeping the floor. He put the broom away after sweeping the 'dirt' out the door. Boden looked at me as I stood.

The look on his face said that he was done talking. "I appreciate you talking with me, Mr. Boden." I held out my hand again.

"Sure."

Boden motioned to go out the back door and we exited the house. Scruffy at Boden's heels. The back yard was just as fastidiously maintained as the front. I was impressed with the landscaping and said so.

"Well…" Boden's eyes lit up in pride. "Now that I'm retired, I have a lot of time on my hands. My wife always liked flowers and such, so I got in the habit of putting in a garden for her. It just grew from that. She was sick for the longest time. She was even bed ridden for about a year. After she died, I had less to do in the house and all, and this sort of became an obsession." He glanced around at all the plants, bushes and trees. "I'm most proud of my roses." He pointed to an area where the flowers were still in bloom near the house. Yellows, red, pink and white blooms not only graced our eyes but blessed our noses.

"Very pretty."

"Thanks." As we walked to the front of the house, he informed me of the various plants and shrubs. Boden knew a lot about plants.

"Well, thanks for the information. If you think of anything else you forgot tonight, don't hesitate to call me," I said.

Boden nodded and waved as I drove off.

I chuckled. I really didn't learn anything tonight, but it seemed that maybe I brightened a lonely man's life just a little. Boden had positively bloomed as he spoke of his flower beds and lawn.

On a whim, I cruised the Meddleson neighborhood again. I stopped in front of the vacant Meddleson house and stared at it. The house practically spoke to me. Something had happened here. Justice needed to be served. The question was who had done it? And why?

Did Simon murder his mom for the six hundred dollars that had been in her 'strong box'? Surely her life was worth more than that? And what of the credit cards? Simon wasn't stupid enough to think that he could use them after her death? And why if he did, were they found in his room on his TV? And why did he come back? I shook my head. *Something didn't make sense here.*

Something was missing.

CHAPTER 5

I jerked awake. Someone had screamed. As I slowed my heart, I realized that it was my scream. Tears flowed unchecked down my face. I wiped at them but it did no good. After several deep breaths, I could feel the terror and fear retreating.

As I swung my legs off the side I saw my son's favorite stuffed rabbit lying next to my pillow. I snagged Petey as tears flowed again and cuddled him in tight to my chest.

"I'm so sorry, Robbie. I love you."

The soft velvety plush of Petey made me feel like I was cuddling Robbie. His curly brown hair. His intense blue eyes which everyone said came from me. I rubbed Petey against my cheek. My only connection now to Robbie.

With a last rub, I reverently placed him back on the pillow and stood. My right leg twinged but didn't dump me to the floor, my other reminder of the car accident that I had survived.

I rarely slept through the night, unless I was exhausted. Trudging to the kitchen, I grabbed a glass of water and plopped down on the stool. The dark, which was usually a comfort, made me feel lonely. I ached for my son, and even for my rat-bastard husband.

The street light was the only lighting in the room and as I looked around, I saw a card on the kitchen counter, near the phone. A tiny shaft of warmth crept into my heart.

Max's card. A card just saying hello.

I cocked my head as the warmth grew. It was the third time that Max's card had eased my pain. I jumped up and grabbed the portable phone next to it. I searched through the list and found his number.

Wait. It's after four in the morning. Two California time. I gently put the phone back, then tapped it once. *Thanks, Max. Thanks for cheering me up. Again.*

With a much lighter feeling, I went back to bed.

***

Early the next morning I booted up the computer. The Texas correctional facility where Devon Miles was incarcerated showed that he was out on parole. Yesterday. I picked up the phone and dialed Roma's number. Waiting for an answer, I thought about the Meddleson murder again.

Where is the dog, Winnie? No one seemed to care that the little dog had disappeared. I frowned and made a mental note to call animal control.

According to the police reports, Ruth Meddleson was found strangled, laying in the middle of the living room. A large cut on her head accounted for all of the blood. The room had been recently cleaned, along with part of the kitchen. The cops suspected it was cleaned after she was murdered. The rest of the house was dusty and dirty. And not many fingerprints anywhere. Those on the scene were all confirmed to be either Ruth's, Simon's or several of the neighbor's fingerprints. Those neighbors all had visited Ruth recently, including Earl Boden, Estella Beaverton, Eugenia Hamilton, and Frank and Mary Allen. Obviously, Simon had cleaned up after himself.

Roma's answering machine picked up. I waited and left a message. Then I listened to the quiet of the empty office. No one was in but me. Switching screens on the computer I started working on another project. But my brain skipped back to Ruth Meddleson.

Why had only the living room and part of the kitchen been clean? Simon denied doing it. *And why would he clean up, if he had done it?* His fingerprints would be in the room since he lived there. *Is this a case of him feeling guilty after the fact? Is this that 'caring' thing that some murderers do after realizing what had happened? It must be.*

I could mentally picture the murder scene. I frowned. I'd have to ask Rich, but strangling a person was usually an act of passion, which didn't denote a premeditated thought. Yet, the cleanliness belied that. Not only did Simon clean the living room but he then drove to St. Louis. *Why? Puzzling. And then he came home?*

Everyone was sure it was Simon, but what if it was someone else? The cops had focused on Simon as the most logical suspect. Even we were approaching it as such. Viking had asked us to find a flaw in the police investigation, meaning that we were to discredit the cops.

Like Rich, I wasn't real happy with it either. I had grown up with cops in the family. My father had retired after 25 years on the force. All of us kids grew up with 'cop' blood in our veins.

But what if the cops hadn't looked for anyone else? It wouldn't be the first time that the police had focused on the wrong person. *Most of the evidence did suggest that Simon was the murderer but....*

I needed to look at this as not trying to get Simon off the hook, but to discover who had killed Ruth Meddleson. Maybe if I took a harder look at Ruth herself....

Three hours later, I sat in Vincent Viking's large mahogany and brass conference room for a discussion of the progress on Simon's case. I clenched my fist under the table. This reminded me so much of my late husband's conference room that I had to keep reminding myself where I was.

Rich tapped my arm. "Okay?" The concern is his eyes spoke volumes. John's attention was on me too. The rest of the assistant attorneys and other clerks in the room were busy scribbling on pads or otherwise occupied.

"Fine."

"Liar." Rich's concerned look stayed. "What?"

"Reminds me of Craig's office."

"Ah!" Rich patted my arm as the door opened and Viking hurried in with another person in tow. Everyone wore suits and ties but us. We were dressed more casually. John and Rich both had on dress shirts but no ties and I was dressed in my usual polo shirt and jeans.

I suppressed a shudder. Vincent wore the same style of clothing as Craig had. I guess all successful attorneys dressed similarly. My dead husband had been an attorney in Maryland with two of his classmates. They had finally made it to the big times after struggling for only a couple of years.

"Sorry, I'm late," Vincent said. "Judge Walton called an emergency meeting in regards to another case." He sat down and smiled, loosening his tie and making himself comfortable.

One of his associates passed him a large cup as another slid a file folder across the table. He took a drink and opened the file. After scanning it, he grimaced. "Okay, Ross, do up another request for the information. I'll need to call Judge Tangleman to see why he denied this one." Vincent shook his head. After a couple of more seconds, he looked at us. He smiled but the tone in his voice said he was not having a very good day. "Tell me you found something."

Rich smiled a 'sorry' at him. "Not much in the way of good news, Vincent."

Viking let out a sigh and motioned for him to speak.

"So far all of Tom's work is on the money. I've looked over all of the paperwork and there isn't a mistake anywhere. I have a call into the coroner's office about the autopsy, but their case looks strong."

"Yeah. I didn't figure Hawkings messed up, but I had to check. Thanks for giving it a critical eye, Rich. I know it was tough on you being friends with Tom." Viking turned to John. "Anything in St. Louis?"

John hesitated before speaking. "I'm not sure." He paused for a few more seconds. "None of Simon's 'friends' would verify he was there the night in question. The only things I could verify were Punky's address, his real name, and the names of the girls. All three denied he was there. No one at the club remembers him."

"So Punky-"

"Jeffery Ledbecker," John interrupted.

Viking continued without a break, "Jeffery Ledbecker was at the night club that Simon mentioned, but won't verify that he was with Simon."

"That's correct. Ledbecker was very nervous when I spoke with him. He claims he was alone."

"And no one saw Simon's car?"

"No."

"Any idea why this guy, or anyone else, is refusing to substantiate Simon's whereabouts?"

"No one even wants to admit knowing him."

Vincent shook his head in frustration as he scribbled some notes. "Okay. The neighbors." He turned to me.

"Won't give me the time of day. My impression is that they're happy Simon's in jail."

"Yeah. We figured that it would be a lost cause."

"But I did run into an older man who gave me some background on Simon's life but nothing about the murder." I looked around the table as the other associates were scribbling notes too. I wondered what they were writing about. None of us had said anything of importance.

Vincent sighed. "Rich, what about the forensic accountant?"

"Still working on it. He said that Ruth Meddleson had several banking accounts besides the one that the police mentioned in the report. One an off-shore account. He wanted me to ask you, if you knew, about them. Perhaps Simon would know."

"Why?"

"Freddy, the accountant, mentioned that one of the accounts had a very large sum of money that fluctuated at times. He's trying to track the money and its source, but he thinks right now that they were all cash deposits."

"How much are we talking here?"

"Freddy mentioned that when Mrs. Meddleson died she had six hundred and seventy five thousand in one of the accounts. He's still tracking the other two. It's harder going since they're off shore accounts. He's supposed to be getting me what he's found tomorrow. I'll bring it by when we get it."

"If we need him to testify, how many days notice does he need?"

"As many as possible."

"Where did you say he lived again?"

"Florida."

"And he's testified before in court?"

"Yeah. We used him a couple of times when I was still on the force. He's since retired from full time, but he likes to keep his hand in things."

"Good. I'll have one of my associates ask Simon when they visit him this afternoon." The attorney turned to one of the males seated near him. "Do it today."

"Yes, sir."

"Anything you want us to do?" Rich asked.

"Keep working on it as you feel best. Just let me know when you get to the specific number of hours we agreed on. I'll decide then if we should continue." He paused. "Anything else?"

No one spoke up.

"Okay then…" Viking glanced at his watch. "I've got another meeting in half an hour. How about we talk again on Friday to see where to go? Sound good, Rich?"

Rich agreed and we left the conference room. As we walked back to the office, Vikings office wasn't far from ours or the court house, we were all silent. Rich turned to John. "How were the people reacting in St. Louis when you talked to them?"

"Scared."

"Why?"

"Got me," John admitted. He frowned. "I'm going back down tomorrow night, if nothing comes up here. I've got a couple of really shady contacts that I couldn't reach the last time. Maybe they'll know more about what's going on."

"Strange."

"To say the least," John commented.

"What do you want me to do?" I asked as we reached the office.

"Run the names again. Dig deeper. Try the phone numbers again," Rich said, holding the door open for me. "I hate to say this but-"

I grunted, giving him a dirty look. "Go talk to the neighbors again. I knew you were going to say that."

Both Rich and John laughed. Pam held up phone messages for all of us.

"And," Pam smiled. "Mel got a big bouquet."

I frowned. "From?"

Pam chuckled. "I put them on your desk."

With a puzzled look at the two guys, I headed for my office. Sure enough, there was a huge vase of cut flowers in the middle of my 'desk'.

The deep red roses contrasted with white Asiatic lilies. With just a touch of greenery, the flowers accented a red matching vase with small red roses at the base. The light fragrance lingered in the room.

My breath caught. They were beautiful. *Who would have sent this?* I saw the card and grabbed it.

John and Rich stood in the doorway.

I read the note, a smile creeping on my face. A warm feeling settled in my heart. I looked at the flowers again and the smile increased. *He's done it again.*

"Who sent them?" Rich asked.

"Max Bauer."

John and Rich smiled at each other in a conspiratorial way. Male-communication that we mere females were never meant to know. Rich chuckled. "Why?"

I smirked. "None of your business."

Rich laughed and left. John shook his head and walked away.

I laid the note down and looked closely at the flowers. They must have cost a lot. I stepped back, admiring them. My heart beat faster as I thought about Max.

Max Bauer had been involved with my first case at Security Investigations. He was the investigating officer on two of the murders, and we became friends. He had expressed an interest in being more then friends, but I had stopped him. I hadn't been ready yet to get into another relationship. I'm still grieving for my family.

The car accident that had claimed my husband had also taken my only son of five. Then I moved home to Quincy, six months after. I wasn't ready for anything beyond friendship. Max had waited, but finally he left after getting a job offer back in his home state of California.

We had spoken on the phone several times in the past few weeks, not to mention the card, and I was beginning to regret his leaving. He was a great guy. Mitch had informed me after I had gotten out of the hospital from the incident, that Max had fallen hard for me. I still wasn't quite ready for a full blown relationship yet, but it would have been fun to hang out with Max.

I moved around the table and was almost seated when Rich sprang back into the room, grabbing the card off the desk.

"Hey!" I half stood in response.

Rich quickly read the note. "Ah, isn't that sweet, Sis," he said as he laid it back down. "Hey, John. Max was thinking of Mel and just wanted to let her know that he missed her." Rich puckered his lips and made kissing noises. "So sweet. I think I'll go vomit." Rich left making gagging noises.

I could hear John laughing in his office.

"Sicko," I called to my brother.

Rich stuck his head back into my office with a big brotherly smile. "He's a nice guy. You could do a lot worse."

"I know. I just don't know if I'm ready."

Rich nodded in understanding. "You're doing fine, Mel. Take your time. Max understands." He winked and left with a light tap on the door frame.

"Yeah," I said softly. I swallowed and wiped at my eyes to stop the tears from forming. I so missed my Robbie. I glanced down at the phone messages. I had two. One was from Earl Boden. *Interesting.* The other phone message was from an unexpected source. My eyebrows rose into my hair.

Bart Hessor.

CHAPTER 6

Bart Hessor.

I stared at the paper. All it said was that he had called. He hadn't left a phone number or any message. I frowned. *What should I do?* I didn't want to encourage him, but he had sort of saved my life. I had phoned him shortly after leaving the hospital to thank him for helping the cops. He hadn't been home, luckily.

The problem came from the fact that Hessor is one of the major drug dealers in town. Not confirmed of course, but everyone knew he was. And, we had a history.

As high school kids we had dated and hung out. Recently, I had run into Bart and found out that he still had 'a thing' for me. He had made it very clear that he still wanted to get to know me better.

If he had a more respectable job, I might consider being friends with him, but that just couldn't happen. Still, I did owe him. It was only because of him that Max and John had found me and captured the murderer.

I sighed, looked up his number then dialed.

"Hello." Bart's voice was very business-like.

"Hi, Bart. It's Mel."

"Mel!" Bart was smiling, I could tell. "How are you doing? All healed?"

"Yeah. I'm fine. Pam said you called."

"I did. I've been out of the country and only got your call today. You're welcome, Mel. I'm glad you got him and he didn't hurt you."

"Yeah, me too."

"You owe me now," he said it sort of joking but I could detect another tone too, maybe arrogance.

"I guess you could look at it that way." I wasn't real happy making this call. And if Rich found out, he'd beat me. Rich hated Bart with a passion. My brother had tried for years to catch Hessor doing *anything* illegal.

"Tell you what, Mel. I'll let you off the hook if you buy me a beer." The slick tone was back in his voice.

I almost sighed. "Sure. When?"

"Tonight?"

"Uh, sure I guess. Where?"

"My bar. Say after nine."

"Okay." We exchanged pleasantries and hung up.

I stared at the phone. *Why had I done that?* I certainly didn't want to date him, and I knew from experience that he would get the wrong idea. I shook my head.

I reached for the phone again and dialed Roma's number. I hadn't heard from her all day. I left another message on her machine figuring that she wouldn't pick up. As I turned on the computer to run Devon's name through the various data bases like DMV, other state agencies, and even Googling his name, trying to pick up where he was, I dug in my purse for my address book.

I dialed another number. Again, I got an answering machine. "Hi Max, it's me. I got your flowers today. Thanks. They're awesome. You brightened my day. I miss you too. Talk to you later." I smiled as I hung up the phone. He made me feel something I hadn't felt in a long time. Treasured.

I settled into doing the data base thing. Devon didn't have any new address that I could find. He hadn't applied for any sort government assistance or anything. So far he was a no-show anywhere. I put him aside and started back on the Simon case. I still had five names to run.

An hour later, Rich stood in my doorway, a stack of papers in his hand and a smile. When he smiled like that, I knew it was more work. "What?"

"More employee checks." He hefted the paperwork in his hand.

We'd taken on several firms in the area as clients to run employee background checks. It was usually my job. I just pointed to a corner near him. "I just sent you via the net the last of the profiles on the Simon case. Any other names you need me to run before I start on the employee backgrounds?"

"Not right now."

"Also…" I stopped Rich as he turned to leave. "I haven't heard from Roma today. And Devon is a no-show in any of the data bases. What do I do about Roma?"

Rich leaned on the doorpost to think. "Have you left a message for her to call?"

I nodded.

"Hmmm… Okay, give her a bit more time. If she hasn't called by four, track her down. If Devon got out yesterday, it might not take him long to find her, if he is as resourceful as he sounds. When you find her, call me and we'll set up a time to get together with John to discuss the case."

"Got it." I looked at the stack of papers. "How soon on the employee checks?"

"The company gave us two weeks but, as usual, as soon as possible."

"You got it." I smiled. "I'll start on them today." My smile turned wry at him. "Guess I won't get to go and talk with the Meddleson neighbors today or tomorrow."

"It's probably better to give them a couple days break anyway. Your nosiness can get annoying. I'd hate to have a law suit for harassment." He walked out, smug.

"Harass? What're you talking about?" I called out to him. "I'm loveable."

"Like a porcupine."

"A cuddly porcupine."

John's laughter floated down the hall. "Gotta love siblings," he said loud enough for us to hear.

"Bite me," I called out to John.

"Bring it on, Mel," John said.

I picked up the phone and placed a call to Mr. Boden. "Hi, Mr. Boden. This is Mel Addison. I'm returning your phone call."

"Oh yes. I called because I was talking with Estella Beaverton who lives near Ruth." He paused.

I nodded to myself as I pulled the first of the employee applications from the pile. "Un huh."

"She said that she heard Ruth and Simon arguing lots of times."

I stopped looking at the application. "When?"

"A couple of days before and the day of the murder."

"What were they arguing about?"

"She didn't tell me and I didn't want to push her."

I frowned. "Will she talk to me?"

"I doubt it."

"Hmmm…"

"You don't by any chance play Canasta, do you?" There was a hopeful tone in his voice.

"I haven't in a long time. Why?" I used to play with a spinster Aunt when she had been laid up in the hospital, but that had been years ago.

"Well, she might loosen up around you if we got in a game. I know she's missing the bi-weekly Canasta games we used to play with Ruth. Stella doesn't play Bridge anymore, so she's been lost without another person to play cards with and only two players isn't as much fun."

Somehow I figured it wasn't just Stella that was missing the games, I smiled. "When do you usually play, Mr. Boden?"

"Tonight. I was planning on heading to her house around six. We usually play until eight or nine. I like to be inside my house by dark. I just thought that it might help you out."

"Sure. That would be great. I'll bone up on my Canasta rules before then. Where do you play?"

"At Stella's house. She's been having trouble with her knees lately. Can't get around much."

"Okay. I'll see you tonight around six then."

I headed to Rich's office. "Hey."

Rich smiled. "There's the prickly porcupine."

"I said cuddly." I smiled. "I just talked with Mr. Boden. He pimped me out for a card game to get information from one the neighbors."

Rich laughed. "Mel, the card shark. What game?"

"Canasta."

"At least you know how to play it."

"True." It was a thing that the family teased me about since childhood. I was a natural at cards. Any card game. I was a killer poker player. In my youth, no one would play me, in anything. "One of the old ladies heard Ruth and Simon arguing the day she was killed."

Rich's eyebrows lifted into his hair. "And?"

"That's all for now. I'll try and dig some info out of the old lady tonight."

"Good. Hey, it might be a good thing if you let her win."

"What fun is that?" I smiled smugly. Everyone knew three things about me. I was stubborn. I was pig-headed. And, I was competitive.

I hurried home to grabbed a quick sandwich as I pulled out a beat up copy of my Rules of Card Games book. It instantly came back to me. *This might even be fun. I haven't played cards in ages.*

As I reached for my drink of Kool-aid, a throw back to my days with Robbie, I chuckled, remembering the one of the times I had played cards. It had been with Craig's partners. And the game was poker.

I had started out playing conservatively, but after the 'boys' had laughed at me a couple of times, I stopped being nice. I ended up winning a great deal of money. Needless to say, I was not invited back for poker night. Ever.

The phone rang.

"Hi. I didn't think I would catch you at home."

The warmth hit me like a downy quilt in the winter. "Max! Thanks again for the flowers."

"Not a problem. I was riding my bike yesterday and thought of you and the ice cream cone incident."

I chuckled. "That was fun."

"Yeah." He paused. "Have you given any thought to coming out to visit me?"

My smiled faded a bit. "Max, uh, not yet. I, uh…"

"Okay." I could tell he was still smiling. "Just reminding you to keep the option open."

I glanced at the clock on the wall. I needed to be heading out soon to be there on time. I'd hate to miss a chance at getting some information. "I'm still working on me, Max. Soon. I promise."

"I'll be waiting."

"Look Max, I hate to cut this short but I have a meeting with someone and if I'm late she might not talk to me. I really need to be in her good graces."

"A case at work?"

"Yeah."

"Sounds important."

"Yeah. No one in the neighborhood will talk to me and I finally got an 'in' with Canasta. If I can get her to talk during it, maybe I can learn something."

I heard Max sigh. "Another murder case?"

"Sort of. And no, I didn't find this body." I took the last drink of my Kool-Aid. "The defendant's attorney hired us to check up on the cop's case. But this was a close neighbor. She might have heard or seen something. A guy I met talked her into letting me play cards with them. If I play my cards right..." I heard him groan at my bad pun. "Sorry about that, I couldn't resist."

"That was really bad, Mel."

I chuckled. "I know. Anyway, she might talk to me."

"The snooping sneak strikes again."

I chuckled even more. "Something like that."

"Well, I'll let you go then. Give me a call sometime when you aren't busy or investigating a dead body."

"I will. Thanks again for the flowers and the call Max." I was smiling so hard my facial muscles started hurting.

"You're more than welcome." His voice got snuggly. "See you. Take care."

I hung up the phone and tapped it. Max was a great guy. I felt all warm and fuzzy. "Canasta," I said to myself and hurried out the door.

I stopped downstairs at the bar. I live above the Full Moon Tavern owned by my Dad and my little brother Cameron. I occasionally work for them or play waitress if they get too busy, but since I started working full time for Rich, it's been less and less. It's a cool place, heavy on family atmosphere. Dad was watching TV since there were only a couple of people in right now.

He turned his head and smiled. "Hi. Want something to drink?"

I leaned on the bar in front of him. "Nah, I'm heading out. I just wanted to let you know that the refrigerator's acting up again."

Dad sighed. He'd tried several times to fix it himself. But since it came with the apartment, it was his problem, not mine. "Okay. Guess it's time for a new one. Want anything specific? Any special color?"

"Nope, just as long as it keeps things cold."

He nodded. "You haven't been down in a few days. How are things?"

I sat down on a stool, sensing this was one of those 'family question and answer periods'. "Fine. I still have my moments but okay, I guess."

"Dot wants you to come over for supper one of these nights."

Mom was in another smothering mood. I'd been avoiding her like a bad cold. "Must I?"

"Yes."

"Okay." Now I did sigh. "I'll call and see when is best."

Dad smirked. "You act like it's worse than getting a root canal coming over to visit us."

"She... she's driving me insane. The other day she wanted me to go through a bunch of pictures of.... Then she wanted me to 'talk' about-"

"She's just trying to help, Sweetie." He only used the 'Sweetie' card when I was in trouble or he was trying to get me to do something I didn't want to do.

"I know but- Ugg!" I shook my head as I stood. "I'm fine."

Dad squeezed my hand.

"I know." I squeezed back and headed out, throwing a 'see ya' over my shoulder.

CHAPTER 7

"Estelle Beaverton, Melissa Addison," Earl Boden introduced us as we stood in the living room of her house. It was a typical bungalow house. There were doilies everywhere in the brown and gold colored interior, and the smell reminded me of Grandma's house.

I smiled nicely and shook her hand. She gave me a very puzzled look when I had walked in with Mr. Boden. She was one of the people who had basically slammed a door in my face.

"Mel plays Canasta and agreed to sit in with us," Boden said, moving to her side and wrapping her hand around his arm. He escorted her into the dining room. "I thought since you haven't played in awhile that you would enjoy tonight."

Mrs. Beaverton looked over her shoulder at me as I followed them into the room. "Yes, but I didn't expect-"

"Now, Stella," Earl said in a very smooth tone.

I tried to hide my smile. Boden was a cool operator. I bet he'd been a lady killer in his younger days. He still had the moves and he was using them on Mrs. Beaverton. I stopped the smile from increasing as I saw her starting to respond to his attentions. The old man still had it in him.

Boden continued without pause, "She's not the enemy. I spoke with this young lady at length the other day. She's just doing her job." He patted her arm as he moved her around the table to a comfortable looking chair. "Besides..." He looked at me and winked. "When was the last time you got to beat such a youngster at cards?"

Mrs. Beaverton laughed and gave him a little slap on the arm. "Earl, you."

Boden gave her a kiss on the cheek as he helped her into the chair. "Just sit and I'll get you a drink." He motioned for me to sit next to her at the square table. "Mel, would you like something to drink?"

"Sure, Mr. Boden. What do you have?"

Earl looked at the lady of the house.

Mrs. Beaverton gave me a serious look. "I have coffee, soda or milk."

I smiled. "A soda would be fine. Thanks."

Earl headed to the kitchen.

I turned to Mrs. Beaverton. "You have a great house, Mrs. Beaverton. I especially like the doll collection. Some look old. Are they?" I noticed as we walked through the living room that she had about thirty porcelain dolls on display. All over, like the doilies. There was even one facing into the corner as if it had been bad. Most people loved to talk about what they are knowledgeable about, especially hobbies.

Her face brightened immediately. "Oh my, yes. My oldest, Hildegard, was passed down to me from my grandmother. She's worth a great deal of money. Most of these..." Stella motioned to the ones in her dining room. "I collected when I was a lot younger."

"They're very pretty. Are they all porcelain?"

"Mostly, but I do have few clay ones. If my knees were better, I'd show you my doll room upstairs." The older lady was now smiling as though I were a long lost friend.

I continued to ask more questions about the dolls in the room until Earl came back in with the drinks. We moved on to the cards. They explained that they played Modern Canasta and Earl shuffled the cards for Stella. The conversation about the dolls continued as we began to play.

Half an hour later, I saw an opening to move the conversation to the topic I wanted to discuss. Stella mentioned something about one time when Ruth Meddleson was playing. "Did Mrs. Meddleson play a good game of Canasta?"

Stella gave me a suspicious look. "Sometimes. A lot of times she was distracted when she played. It was because of Simon, but I think she had a lot of other things on her mind."

I discarded. "Simon sounds like a real handful."

Boden nodded in agreement as he picked up a card off the draw pile then discarded it. "He just needed a man's hand. Always in trouble with the law."

Stella shook her head as she looked closely at Earl's discard. She picked up a card off the draw pile instead. "I don't think that would have helped at all. Simon was just wild. Did anything he pleased since he was little. A wild child."

"And he had the filthiest mouth," Boden said watching the older lady meld her cards on the table. "Always disrespectful toward Ruth too."

"Oh my, yes. What a mouth." Stella nodded, finally she discarded. "He said things I never, well, they were just filthy."

"How did the two of them get along?" I asked picking up the card she had just laid down. I shuffled some cards around in my hand and put a wild card on the discard pile to freeze it. I gave a little shrug with a slight smile at the look of disgust on Mrs. Beaverton's face at my actions.

"That's twice now that you've frozen the pile," Stella said, her lips pursed.

I nodded.

"You're not inexperienced at playing Canasta, are you?"

"I was taught by my Aunt. She was a very aggressive player." I inclined my head toward the pile. Aunt Dorothy taught me all of her tricks, then I made up more of my own.

Stella laughed. "I can tell." She watched as Earl discarded a six that she could have picked up if I hadn't frozen the pile. She gave me another dirty look then picked up from the draw pile. "Usually they got along fine. Although he was a rebel and a trouble maker, Simon was sometimes nice to Ruth."

"Unless it had to do with money," Earl chimed in.

"True," Stella said as she discarded. "They did argue all the time over money. Simon wanted it and Ruth generally wouldn't give it to him."

"Did she have a lot of money?"

"Ruth? Heaven's no. Always just scraping by." Stella chuckled. "But she always found money for a little nip when we played. Of course, I haven't been able to drink since my heart attack."

Earl gave her a look of surprise. "Since when? Stella, don't lie to the girl." Earl turned to me. "Bea always helped Ruth with her 'special coffees'." He winked.

I smiled. Mr. Boden would call her Bea, I guessed a shortened form of Beaverton, or Stella depending on how much he was flirting with her. "So Simon really did love his mother."

Stella paused at my statement, looking at me closely. I could tell she was sizing me up. "Well, yes he did. When they weren't fighting, he almost doted on her." Stella concentrated on her cards for a few seconds. "I remember when he got her Winnie for her birthday."

I kept the surprise off my face. *Simon doted on her? And he had been the one to get her the dog? Then he strangled her to death?* I moved some cards around in my hand. *Odd.*

Stella continued to speak, "Ruth was so enthralled with Winston. His nickname was Winnie, you know. She treated that dog better than most people do kids. I swear sometimes I think she thought it was another kid. Simon was so happy that she liked the Shih Tzu so well."

"Where is the dog now?" The thought just occurred to me that I had forgotten to check with animal control.

Stella paused and looked at me puzzled. "I don't know. Earl, do you?"

He nodded as he took a drink of coffee. "I think the police gave him to Ruth's niece in Canton."

"Was Simon ever jealous of the dog and her attentions to it?" I asked as Earl discarded.

Stella shook her head. "He was amused by it, I think." She gave me a disgusted look since the discard could have given her another canasta. She grabbed a card off the draw pile instead. "You know, I think he was actually happy that Ruth had found something to love besides him."

"So, he wasn't the jealous type?"

"Not about Winnie," Stella answered. "Earl, could you get me a refill on my coffee?"

"Sure, Bea." Earl stood immediately and took her cup to the kitchen.

Stella gave him a sweet smile as she followed his movements out of the room. "He's such a sweet man."

She had a sexy look in her eye. Suddenly I wondered if Earl and her didn't have something going on. I almost chuckled, then as I thought about it further, I didn't want to know any more. It would be like walking in on your grandparents. Not something I really wanted to know about. "Mr. Boden is a nice man. I saw his yard. He takes great care of his lawn."

"His roses are his babies. Besides, Scruffy. Talk about doting on a dog!" She smiled, then her tone turned puzzled. "I wonder why Earl didn't take Winnie. He always took him for walks with Scruffy. Oh well, at least the dog has a nice home."

"You said that Ruth and Simon argued all the time over money."

Stella nodded as Earl came back into the room. "Yes, it always bothered Ruth when they argued. Simon was forever needing money and she was upset that she couldn't give it to him."

"He would have just blown it anyway," Earl piped in.

"Really?" I asked, hoping to keep this flow of information going. I hadn't learned anything new yet but it was interesting hearing more about them.

Stella nodded as she contemplated her cards. The gossip in her seemed to be blossoming. "Oh my, yes. He was always gambling. Lost a whole lot of money and even his car one time. At least that's what Ruth told me. He was in big trouble with some guys in St. Louis for awhile there. Then he must have hit the ponies or something, because the next month he not only had a new car but also bought Ruth her new car."

Earl agreed. He melded his cards on the table.

I was the only one still holding all my cards. Stella already had one canasta and was close to getting another. It was risky what I was doing, but if it worked, it would pay off.

"Then he blew that, as usual," Earl added as he discarded.

Stella frowned at the card, she could have made a third canasta and probably gone out if she could have picked it up. "Ruth told me right before she died that he was in trouble again."

My eyes flashed to her face. I tried to contain my excitement. "Yes?"

Stella concentrating on the cards. "She didn't say what about, but he needed money again. They argued the afternoon she was killed. I had stopped by to give her one of my medical books. You know, that kind that explains

44

medical terms. She'd called earlier in the day and asked if she could borrow it. Anyway, as I walked up I heard them arguing."

"About?"

"I don't know for sure. I assume money. That's all they ever argued about."

"What did you hear them say?"

"Hmmm…" Stella was looking at her cards. "Simon said something about that she needed to protect herself better and why did she always get into these things. Or something like that. Then he said he'd deal with it. She said that she would take care of it, that it wasn't any of his business." Stella shook her head. "Then it escalated into calling each other names. I went back home and decided to give her the book the next day."

I watched as she discarded. I almost smiled, just the card I needed.

"No one answered the next morning."

Boden and I both looked at Stella.

The little old lady was rearranging her cards in her hand. Finally at the silence in the room, she looked up. A sad look was on her face, tears growing in her eyes. "I guess she was already dead then, it was before Mary Alice went by."

I reached out and patted her hand. "I'm sorry, Mrs. Beaverton. I didn't mean for you to relive it."

She sniffled.

From what I had read in the police reports, no one had even approached the house until Mrs. Allen looked into the window around noontime. *Interesting.* Maybe one of the other neighbors had more information too.

I picked up the whole discard pile, since I had two of the discarded cards in my hand, and with a grin at the disgusted looks on their faces, melded onto the board. With what was in my hand and in the discard pile, I ended up with three Canastas and went out, leaving both Stella and Earl holding cards.

After counting up their loses, Stella turned to me with a new respect in her eyes. "You're very good at this game. Would you consider playing us again? And do you play Bridge? I'd start playing again if you were my partner."

I chuckled. "Thanks. And yes, I'd like to play again with you. I do not play Bridge. I never got into the game."

"Too bad," Stella said. "I think if you and I played as a team, we could beat Earl and Frank hands down." She smiled wryly at Boden.

Earl laughed. "If I knew she was this sharp, I'd have thought twice about inviting her."

I laughed, shuffling the cards. This would probably be the last hand. Not only was it getting late, but someone would win with the next hand.

***

I walked into Su Casa's at nine and looked around. It was kind of crowded but not packed. Su Casa's is an upscale Mexican bar on Broadway; typical

Mexican décor but not over done, nice and inviting. Slightly over priced beers but other than that the only bad thing about it is its owner, Bart Hessor.

I gave a quick glance around but he wasn't there. With a sigh, I stepped up to the bar and ordered a soda. No beer tonight. Not with Bart. I needed to be in control of all of my faculties.

The bartender set my drink in front of me. "Are you Mel Addison?"

I didn't stop the look of surprise on my face. "Yes. How did you know?"

He smiled. "My name is Matt. Mr. Hessor gave me a description and asked me to watch out for you tonight. He called and wanted me to tell you that he's running late. He'll be here in about an hour."

"Okay." I reached for my wallet.

Matt shook his head. "Your drinks are on Mr. Hessor."

"Thanks, Matt."

With a tip of his head, he moved off to wait on other customers. I got settled on the bar stool. As I did my mind went back to the conversation at the card game.

Mrs. Beaverton had knocked on the door early the day after Ruth had been killed. I would need to pin her down to a time at the next card game. *What had Simon and Ruth been arguing about? And why had Ruth asked for a medical book from Beaverton? Did Simon know? Maybe one of Vincent Viking's associates could ask him for me. Simon loved his mom. He doted on her, but he killed her. By strangling? That didn't sound right.* A voice interrupted my thoughts.

"Mel? Mel Addison?"

I turned at the male voice to find a rather portly, short, balding man giving me that 'long lost friend' look. I ran his face through all of my memories but came up blank. I smiled hesitantly. "I'm sorry but…"

"Kenny Crandle." He stuck out his hand.

"Kenny!" Now I remembered him. He had been my lab partner in chemistry class in high school. "How are you?"

"Doing good. You look great!" Kenny leaned next to me on the bar.

From his attitude, he was going to hit on me. So I adopted a more formal posture, one that said 'I'm not available'. We talked for a short time. Mostly he told me about his business in town. I made nice because he was the only reason I had passed Chemistry class and I owed him that. Twenty minutes later he excused himself to return to his 'buddies' at their table.

I overheard a comment one of his friends made to him, "Man, she is gorgeous. Did you get her number?"

I chuckled as I sipped at my soda. I noticed for awhile they kept looking at me, with Kenny obviously being the big man at the table. It was okay though, I had used him in chemistry class to get an easy grade so it was only fair that now he was capitalizing on knowing me.

For the next hour, I watched the TV. Some soccer game- European if I had to guess. My mind wondered back to Roma. *Where was she?* After leaving

Beaverton's house, I had driven by Roma's, since she still wasn't answering her phone. She hadn't been home. She knew that I was supposed to be checking back in with her, so why wasn't she around? *Too strange.*

After finishing my third soda, I called Matt over. "Tell Bart I'll meet him another day." I left Su Casa's heading home.

I contemplated calling Max but didn't. With a hope and prayer that tonight I didn't wake from bad dreams, I went to bed. Sleep didn't come fast. After a long time, I grabbed Petey and cuddled up. Finally, I dozed.

***

The next morning I drove past Roma's house again before heading into work. Still no one at home. Now I was starting to get worried. *Where was she? And what caused her to disappear like that?*

Rich was at the office when I got there.

I headed directly to his room. "Hey, got a minute, Rich?"

"Sure. By the way, Roma called early this morning..." Rich began.

I let out a breath in relief.

"Yeah. I told her what we found out. She's coming here later in the morning after John's in to talk with us about the situation. Then after lunch John is headed back down to the St. Louis area to dig up more on Simon." He paused. "Did you learn anything from the card game lady?"

"Yeah." I smiled. "Mrs. Beaverton, who lives two houses from the Meddlesons, heard Simon and Ruth arguing the day she was killed."

Rich's eyebrows rose. "That's not in Hawkings' notes."

"She was taking a medical dictionary over to Ruth. Ruth had called her and wanted to borrow it."

"Why?"

"Mrs. Beaverton didn't know." I paused. "Anyway, she left before knocking on the door when she heard them arguing..." I relayed in detail all of the information that Beaverton had told me.

Rich sat back in thought. "Interesting." He was studying his desk top, then he looked up at me with a grin on his face. "Can you learn Bridge? Maybe the other neighbors will open up to you if you play them too."

I screwed up my face. "I hate Bridge. No. But I have already set a date to play Canasta with the two of them again. And I think I'll pop over to her house this afternoon to quiz her more on the argument. Anything else you want me to do on the case?"

Rich shook his head.

"What about the autopsy?"

"Yeah. The head wound was caused by hitting the coffee table as she fell. Simon didn't clean up everywhere. He missed a small spot on the table. Blood and bone were found there. The coroner confirmed the injury. But that wasn't what killed her. She was strangled. The coroner suspects that left alone, she probably would have died from the head injuries but..." He drifted off.

"Is it usual for a strangler to clean up after the fact?" I sat in the chair in front of his desk.

"Sometimes. Depends on the murderer. Some of them will clean up after, say in the case of regret for the action done to a loved one." Rich leaned forward. "Somehow though, I don't see Simon taking that step. Probably had Tom worried too."

"Isn't strangling usually done in a fit of passion?"

"Usually, but not always. Why?"

"What if Simon didn't kill his mom?"

Rich shook his head immediately. "Tom's evidence is strong, even with the couple of loose ends."

"I know but... Where is Winnie?"

"Who?" Rich's eyebrows knitted together.

"Where's the dog?"

"What dog?"

"Ruth Meddleson's dog, Winston?"

Rich sat back staring at me. "Okay, I didn't think of that. Why would the location of the dog mean anything?"

"Simon bought it for his mom. We know he loves her. That was about the only thing I believed in his story at the jail. Did he do something to the dog?" I paused. "Did animal control take the dog?"

"I don't see-"

"Beaverton and Boden were both shocked that the dog was missing. I got the impression that both of the Meddlesons loved the little Shih Tzu. Where is it?"

Rich smiled. "You pick the strangest things to focus on, Mel."

I shrugged.

"I'll call Vincent and have them ask Simon the next time they're in to see him. Okay? Will that make you feel better, you dog lover?"

"Funny, Rich. I just found it a little... odd."

Rich shook his head.

"So, after reading all of the police reports do you think Simon did it?"

"Tom crossed all his I's and dotted his t's. Yeah, I'm convinced Simon did it."

"I don't know, Rich."

"The State still has to prove it, but I'm convinced by Tom's evidence. Vincent's pretty worried too."

I just studied my shoes. *But where is Winnie?*

CHAPTER 8

"So, what are my options?" Roma asked us.

The four of us were seated in the conference room. John was leaning back, listening. He had walked in minutes before Roma showed up.

Rich shook his head. "There's not a lot we can do right now Roma. Until Devon shows up here or in a data base, it's basically a wait and see. At the first letter or phone call, you need to get the police involved. That way it'll be documented. At the first sign of a threat, we'll have you petition for another restraining order."

"But all that will do is make him mad. Again."

"I know, but once that happens, and he's caught, he's violated his parole and he can be incarcerated again."

"What?"

"His parole stipulates he cannot leave his jurisdiction in Texas. If he's here, he's in violation of his parole. Then it's only a matter of having the cops pick him up." Rich smiled. "Just sit tight and go about your normal routine. Mel will pop over occasionally to see you at home. Any contact from him at all, any, call us. John and I will drive by your house on a prearranged schedule, too. We'll see if we can find him."

Roma gave a slight, if not hesitant, nod.

"If you see him or even suspect he's around, call. One of us will be over there lickety split." Rich handed her a card with all of our cell numbers. "It's all we can do for now."

Roma took a deep breath. "Okay. I guess it's a relief knowing that someone cares and is trying to help." Shortly after wards, she left.

I headed to my office and called animal control. No, the police hadn't called them that day to get a dog. I thanked them and then did as they suggested, I called the local pound. No, they didn't have a dog dropped off around that time. And they would remember a Shih Tzu, apparently they were in high demand and easily adopted out.

I frowned. *Where is the silly little mut?*

"That's a terrible frown, Sis." Rich was leaning on the doorpost looking in at me.

"The dog is a no show anywhere."

"So? Maybe it ran away."

I made a face.

"Ask Simon. Vincent's having a meeting with him in about an hour. He said it was okay for you to be there. Go ask about the stupid dog. It'll put your mind at ease."

"Yeah, sure."

Pam announced that I had a call. Rich left as I picked up the phone.

"This is Mel."

"How's the snooping going?"

Max. "Slow. I'm missing a dog."

"What?"

"Yeah. Everything makes sense in the case against the client, but the woman's dog is missing. No one knows where it is."

There was a pause on the line. "So?"

"So? Ruth, the dead lady and her son, the suspected murderer, both loved Winnie. But it has disappeared off the face of the earth."

I heard a chuckle.

"Mel, if he killed his mom, he wouldn't have a qualm about killing a dog."

"I don't know."

"Here we go again."

I sighed. "It's the biggest loose end, Max."

"Listen Tiger, in this business not every loose end gets tied. This isn't a novel you know. Who was the Lead Detective?"

"Tom Hawkings."

"He's good, Mel. If he has enough evidence to arrest, then you can bet its Simon."

I didn't respond.

"But hey, I didn't call about that."

"Okay, what is the occasion of this call, Mr. California Policeman."

"Mr. California Detective, Mel. Get it straight." The tone was joking.

"Pardon."

Max laughed. "I was just going to suggest that when you find the little mut, then maybe you'd come out for a visit."

I frowned. I liked Max to be sure, but he was starting to get pushy, again. "Look Max-"

"There's a terrific sale on airline tickets right now. From St. Louis to here…" There was a pause. "I'd even help pay."

"Not now, Max. I'm, I'm still not ready yet."

I heard a slight sigh. "Okay. I'm trying."

"I know." I swallowed back the 'too hard' part. "Look, I appreciate the offer but I'm busy and it's not.... Not now."

"Okay. In that case, can I get you to do me a favor?"

"Sure. I guess."

"Can you mail me some Mississippi mud?"

I got a perplexed look on my face. "What for?"

"I miss the smell." Sarcasm.

I chuckled. Max always made me laugh. "Mud coming up."

Max chuckled too. "Look, I'm due on surveillance in a few minutes. Call me tomorrow when you get time, it's my day off. I miss talking with my favorite snooping sneak."

"Sure, Max. I'll call tomorrow."

"See ya, Tiger."

I still held the phone in my hand, listening to the buzz. He was trying too hard. *How did I tell him to back off without losing him as a friend?*

***

Simon was shown into the jail conference room. He looked a little more haggard than before, maybe just lack of sleep or something. "Where's my attorney?"

I shrugged. "Probably running late. But since I'm here, can I ask you a question?"

Simon ran a hand through his hair. "I remember you, ya know."

"Yeah. Thanks for not saying anything to Rich."

Simon smiled a knowing smile. "Shoot, Mel."

"Actually two." I paused. "Did you kill your mom?"

He immediately shook his head. "I loved Ma." He glanced away quickly. "I'd like ta find the guy who did it though. Then I'd be willing to spend the rest of my life in prison. I'd even call the cops myself after I capped him."

"Why 'him'?"

Simon's head snapped to me.

I could see the gathered tears in the corner of his eyes. They didn't look fake. "Why did you say 'him'?"

He shrugged, sniffling once. With a quick wipe, his eyes were back to normal. "Mom was a pretty tough woman. I doubt a woman could'a done this. She'd of kicked the dog snot outta a woman. I've seen her stand up to some pretty tough guys, too." I could tell he was telling the truth now. "Was that all of the questions, Mel?"

"No. What happened to Winnie?"

"What?"

"Winston. Where is he?"

Simon sat up in his seat more alert. "The cops didn't do something to him, did they?"

I shook my head. "Winnie's not at animal control as he would have been if he was in the house when your mom was found. I even called the pound to see if maybe he ran away and was taken there by someone else." I shook my head. "Did Winnie wear a collar?"

"Yeah. Blue and red leather. Mom had his name stamped on it. Red with a blue kind of design on it." He shook his head then lowered his gaze to the table. "Winnie's gone too."

I just sat there. Simon was truly saddened by the news. This wasn't faked. Or if it was, he was a really good actor. From the past, I'd have to say it was not an act. "Simon…"

He rubbed his eyes before looking up. "Yeah?"

"Would Winnie run away?"

"No. He'd try to protect Mom. He's dead too."

I took a breath as Simon looked me in the eyes. "You weren't at Rascal's, were you?"

"I was in St. Louis."

"At Rascals?"

Simon nodded. Now I knew he was lying.

"I have to tell you that none of us believe you, Simon. We can't get anyone to verify that you were there."

"Not surprising," Simon said matter-of-factly, "I understand." He looked me in the eyes. "I did not kill Mom or Winnie."

"Despite all the evidence, Simon, I believe you."

"You'd be the only one." He paused with a sad look in his eyes. "Thanks, Mel."

The door opened and Viking walked in. He apologized to us then sat down. "This does not look good, Simon."

Simon nodded, almost in defeat.

"I think we should plea bargain. I think I could get it down to voluntary manslaughter. Fifteen to twenty-five years with good behavior." Viking shook his head. "I'm calling off the PIs. I don't want to waste anymore of your money."

Although Simon's head was down, his eyes panned to me. Then he lifted his head, eyes still locked with mine. "Yeah, okay. Talk to the district attorney, but hold off on makin' a deal. Wait."

"Simon, the sooner we make the bargain the better. The evidence is very convincing. They aren't going to deal for long."

Simon glanced from Viking back to me. "I know." He held my eyes. "Just wait."

My gut wrenched. Yes, I did believe he was innocent. I had to keep looking. My head barely moved in a dip, but he understood.

Simon turned his attention back to Viking. "Get rid of the detectives. Hire just Mel."

"What?"

"I only want Mel workin' for me."

"I can't do that, Simon," Viking said with a side glance at me.

"Why not?"

I answered Simon. "I'm not licensed yet."

Simon shrugged then glanced back at Viking. "Fine. Fire the whole lot. I want to hire you Mel. Just you, as a private citizen. And Viking…" Simon turned his beady eyes on his attorney. They were now hard, the eyes of a knowing criminal. "Tell no one. Not even her bosses. I don't trust them, particularly her brother. No offense, Mel."

"I can't, Simon. I will not-"

Simon interrupted him as he stood up. "Fine. Then don't." He stared down at me.

I took a deep breath and looked Simon in the eye. I gave him another miniscule head nod. Unfortunately, I did believe he was innocent. And no matter what anyone else thought, I knew I had to help him. *I had to help him.* I couldn't let an innocent man go to jail, even one with his past. The non-crazy part of my brain was screaming at me that I couldn't go against my brother and everyone else. I rarely listened to it. I knew he was innocent.

"Hold off on the deal, Viking." He turned away from us. "Guard!"

***

I ran by Beaverton's house but she wasn't home so I headed to Roma's that night just to check in with her. After inviting me in, she moved back into the kitchen to finish the dishes. There was a small, decorated cake sitting on the counter, blue flowers on white frosting.

"Have you seen or had any indication that Devon's here in town?" I asked.

"Is there any way to find him?"

"I'm trying. Every morning I check all the data bases for any sign of him. We can usually track people if they aren't trying to hide."

That didn't seem to surprise her as she continued to wash the pans. I didn't know what to say to her so I just sat wondering how I was going to extract myself, graciously.

She turned suddenly and sat down next to me. "I'm so lonely, Mel." Roma slowly dried her wet hands.

I was stunned.

"I can't meet any guys. I'm scared to even make female friends. I'm so scared of Devon. I know he'll show up here." She started crying. "I just want to die sometimes."

I patted her shoulder. I rubbed her back as she sobbed, pulling her onto my shoulder. *What did I say to her?* Anything I thought of sounded trite and stupid.

"You know the worst thing?"

I shook my head as she sat back, wiped her nose with the back of her hand.

"I can't go home. He's threatened my parents before. Today is Dad's birthday. That's his cake. I'm talking to them later on the phone. I can't even go home to celebrate his birthday." She started crying again.

I pulled her into another hug.

After several minutes of letting her cry, she finally pushed off my shoulder. "Thanks. You and the others are the best comfort. I know that he's coming after me. I know he'll be... I just feel that now someone actually believes me besides my parents."

"We do. Call any of us, Roma. Night or day."

She shook her head. "You all have regular lives. I, on the other hand, have no life."

"You will. Just give us time, Roma."

"You've never been stalked. You don't know what it's like."

"True, but we want to help."

Roma wiped her tears again. The phone rang and she jumped in her seat. Her hand went to her chest. "I know that's him. The phone has been ringing every hour."

"Why didn't you tell us?"

"It just started. He hangs up before the answering machine picks up, but I know it's him. I know." She rung her hands as she stood up and paced the room. "He's back. He'll never leave me alone."

The answering machine finally picked up. A female voice. "Roma, Baby, it's just us. It's eight, like you said. Are you there?"

Roma smiled through her renewed tears. "Mom." She hurried over to the phone.

"I'll just leave-"

"Wait. Will you have a piece of cake, Mel?"

I hesitated.

"Please." She picked up the phone. "Hi Mom." Her pleading eyes locked with mine.

I sat back down.

***

What was I doing? I sat at the Full Moon with a beer in hand. It was a slow night. The guys at the other end were arguing over something on the TV. Dad was gossiping at the other end. I sighed and went back to looking at the bar top.

Why did I let Simon get to me? What a loser! But he didn't kill his mom. Of that fact I was certain. And Devon would return to haunt Roma. I was certain of that too after talking with her while we ate cake and ice cream. And now I was stuck in the middle of both cases. Smack in the middle.

I didn't need this. I could feel the roller coaster of emotions starting tonight. I hadn't had this feeling in a week or so, but it was starting early tonight.

"Hey, Mel!" A male voice called from the other side.

I glanced up to see that it was one of the local men in blue. "What?"

"Throw some darts with us. Take our money, like always," Steve Wettle called out to me with a smile. The group of four guys started laughing. The argument was over, the beers were flowing, and the camaraderie being offered was genuine.

"Thanks guys. No." I swallowed down the rest of the beer. I practiced throwing darts all the time when business was slow and I had become almost as good as I had been in my youth. "Not tonight." I got off the stool and gave a slight wave at Dad, who nodded back, deep in conversation.

I exited the bar heading to the back of the building and the stairs that lead up to my apartment. It was a nice night out. The bright stars were twinkling. I stretched as I leaned back looking up into the heavens.

"Mel!"

I turned. Steve Wettle, still a patrol cop like Mitch, had followed me outside. I waited until he moved closer. "I don't want to take your money tonight, Steve."

He chuckled. "Okay. Hey, I've got a question for you."

I waited.

"Uh… I have a couple of tickets to the ball game in St. Louis. I'd feel honored if you'd go with me."

I stared into the hazel eyes of the blond headed cop. There was a look in them that I remembered from the past. But this was more respectful than the usual 'hit on a woman' look.

"Mitch said you might consent to go with me." A hardly noticeable plea was in his tone.

I just looked at him.

"This does not look good for the home team," he said with a small smile.

"Mitch said that, huh?"

He nodded hesitantly.

"Thanks for the offer, Steve-"

"But no," he finished for me. "You know, if you keep turning us down, we'll have to retaliate." It was said with his usual tone of voice, as though I was his best friend's little sister. This was how most of the cops on the force spoke to me.

Larry, Mitch's best friend also a cop, had asked me out last week, using almost the same tone. If I didn't know better, I'd think that Mitch was trying to set me up. "Yeah. Tell Mitch to bite me. I think I'm going to start dating the firefighters for a change. After all, they like to 'play with fire'." I winked.

Steve cracked up laughing. "But we like to use force."

"Firefighters make things *smoke*."

Steve patted me on the shoulder. "You know what they say about firefighter though, they like to play with hoses."

I laughed as we parted ways. Steve headed back into the bar and me up the stairs, still shaking my head. It was a big thing in 'The Moon', as everyone called it, the firefighters and the cops argued and competed over everything. Everything.

As I puttered around the apartment winding down, I chuckled some more. I'd have to have a sister-brother heart to heart with Mitch. I knew what he was trying to do, but I did not want to date. I wanted to be left alone.

Sitting on the edge of the bed that night, my mind wandered back to my dead family. I sorely missed them, especially Robbie. I wanted so much to hold him. To hug him. To kiss him. To hear his laughter.

I started crying. I missed him so much it felt like my stomach was twisted in knots and my heart was bleeding profusely.

I grabbed Petey. I stared at Petey as the tears flowed down my face. "I'm sorry, Petey."

Once more Petey put me to sleep. Petey, my substitute Robbie.

***

I arrived early at work the next morning. I knew Viking was going to call Rich informing him that we were officially off the case. I wanted to make copies of the police reports and other associated paperwork before it was permanently filed. I found it on Rich's desk, all neatly bundled up. Apparently Vincent had already informed Rich. That was good, all of it was waiting for me.

I finished with the last of the papers when Rich walked in. He stopped and stared at me as I put the papers back on his desk.

"We're off the case, as of last night."

"I know, but I also know that Simon is innocent."

"Vincent told me what Simon asked."

Our eyes locked.

"You're not doing this, Mel. We're off the case."

"I know."

"Then why did you just return the file to my desk?"

"Why does it matter?" I asked back in the same tone.

"Doesn't matter what you think or think you know. Doesn't even matter if Simon is innocent. We're off the case."

"That's the third time you've said that. Are you getting old?"

"What are you up to?"

"Nothing." I turned to leave his room.

"Mel…"

I turned back.

"We are off of the case." He stressed every syllable.

"I know." I stressed back to him. I heard him muttering to himself as I left the room. I quickly hid the copies in my pile of paperwork lying on the floor. Tonight, I would study them, at home.

"Hey, Rich…," I called. When he appeared at my door, I continued, "I stopped by Roma's last night. She thinks that Devon is calling her again."

Rich frowned.

"But there's no proof. The phone disconnects before the answering machine picks up and caller ID comes up 'unidentified'. I checked the four calls that happened while I was there."

"Until we can verify it's him, there's no recourse. Neither John nor I have seen him on our runs passed the house."

"What else can we do?"

Rich rubbed his chin. "Let me think on it."

***

I spread the Simon case paperwork on my kitchen counter after work. I grouped it into police reports, lawyer reports, our reports and miscellaneous. Our reports I put back into the file folder. I knew that stuff.

I glanced at the clock, keeping an eye on the time since I was due at the parent's house for supper but I wanted to get a head start on this. The first group I picked up was Vincent's papers.

Not a whole lot new here, except that Simon had changed his story twice. First, he reported to Vincent that he had been in St. Louis and East St. Louis on 'business'. Then he changed his story to include the bit about Rascals and Punky's girlfriend. The rest of the notes were not very informative.

Why had he changed his story? Obviously, he was lying. *Did he think that Punky would have verified his whereabouts? And why wasn't he surprised that we couldn't get anyone to say they had seen him? He didn't even seem upset about it. Hmmm, interesting.*

I reached for the police reports when I remembered that I was supposed to call Max tonight. I grabbed the portable phone with mixed feelings.

I really liked Max, as a friend though. He was pushing for more and I wasn't sure I wanted it. The idea of me being free from my commitment was not something I was comfortable with, yet. I had taken a vow, and although I knew I was released from it, with Craig's death, I couldn't bring myself to date yet. My feelings were still tumbling around. I had still loved the rat-bastard, but…. I didn't know what I wanted… from anything.

"I wondered when you would be calling. Almost thought I'd been stood up." Max's voice was smiling.

"Yeah, well, I was busy." There was a sudden silence on the other end of the phone. "Max?"

"Yeah."

"I thought that my portable winked out on me."

"I can let you go."

I frowned. "I called you."

"Look Mel, if you don't want to talk to me-"

"What gave you that idea?"

"You."

"Oh, the busy thing. Sorry. I have a lot on my mind." I smiled, trying to inject it into my voice. "Things. You know."

"No, I don't."

I sighed. "The truth, Bauer?"

"That's all I've ever asked for."

"I like you, but you're pushing again."

"The plane ticket thing, uh?"

"Yeah."

There was a silence on the other line for a couple of seconds. "The thing is, I like you. I want to spend time with you. I'd fly back there if I had any time off or if there was anything to do there."

I chuckled. "What? Corn fields aren't enough for you?"

Max chuckled too. "Don't forget the smelly Mississippi."

"Now, I take offense. The river smell is an acquired taste. Kind of like the ocean."

"No comparison, Mel. None. The ocean is a clean smell, whereas the muddy Mississippi is a... fishy smell or a..."

I could tell he was really searching for another word, so I finished for him. "Stinky smell? Only when I interrupt your sleep to introduce you to a dead, bloated, decomposing body." One of our previous 'dates'.

Max laughed. "You do make my day."

I smiled. Max was always fun to be with.

"So, have you found the little doggie yet?"

"No. And I'm getting more and more worried. Simon has lied about other things, but I know he didn't kill his mom."

"And you know this how?"

"I can just tell. He's not lying about this."

"This is from your years of experience in law enforcement work, I take it?"

"Bite me, Max. I can just tell. A mom learns these things."

"And your mom radar went up at his lying at the 'other things'?"

"Yeap."

"Thanks. I can make chief now. All I have to do is to hire a bunch of moms to interview suspects. I'll be the most famous police chief ever."

"I'm serious."

"So am I." His tone had turned serious. "I don't mean to get in an argument with you, but if he's lied before, he'll lie again."

"Yeah."

"From what I've heard, it sounds like Simon killed his mom and the little dog too." Max slurped at a drink.

I didn't respond. I knew Simon didn't kill his mom.

"Okay. You're obviously going to pursue this. Do you want me to act as your sounding board?"

"Not with that attitude."

"Fine. I'll be more objective but I won't stop playing devil's advocate." He paused. "You mentioned loose ends last time I spoke with you. List them."

"Winnie."

"It's missing. Move on."

"Simon's a slob. The murder scene was immaculate."

Max slurped some more. "Okay. He cleaned up after the fact. Was he living at her home?"

"Off and on."

"Hmmm… Okay, a puzzler." He paused. "How do you know he's a slob?"

"Police report said his room was a total mess, like a teenagers. His car was filthy. I used to know him."

There was a long sigh from the phone. "Was he another old boyfriend? Is this the cause of your loyalty?"

"No, he wasn't. He was a couple of years behind me in the public high school. He used to occasionally hang out at the campsite down by the river with us." I paused.

"Go on."

"I just remember him vaguely as always being a messy dresser and even unclean. If I remember right, he wasn't good in school either." I thought back to my youth. "He hasn't changed."

"How was the mom killed?"

"Strangled, but with a blow to the head from the coffee table. Coroner says left without medical help, she might have died from it."

"Okay, so he strangled her after a fight and then felt bad about it. Most people love their moms."

My heart froze. My breath froze. Time froze. My mind slipped back in time. I was standing outside my car, my five year old son spoke to me as I put him in his car seat, 'I love you, Mommy.' I could feel tears flowing. It was the last thing he had said to me.

"Mel?" Max's voice was raised. "Mel?"

"Uh, yeah… What?"

"Where did you go?"

"Excuse me?"

"You didn't respond. Are you okay?"

I rubbed my face and eyes to stop the tears. "Yeah. You were saying?"

"Are you okay?"

"Why?"

"You're crying. You sound… far away."

"Sorry. Something you said reminded me of…" I stopped. "Nothing."

"Nothing?" There was a pause then Max's voice got soft. "Robbie, huh?"

I sniffled and wiped at the tears. "Yeah. Sorry."

"Don't apologize. Robbie was your son. I understand." Max paused then continued. "All I meant was that it shows that Simon felt bad. Next loose end, if you want to continue."

"Yeah." I wiped my cheeks dry and shook myself. "Okay, the cops say that Simon took her credit cards and six hundred dollars out of her stash, but the cards were found on his TV in his room. He was supposedly in St. Louis and they had argued about money. He needed money again. On his TV, Max. Not in his wallet or on his person. He claims he didn't know that they were there."

"In plain sight? The money too?" Max's tone had turned incredulous.

"Yeap." I picked up the police reports.

"Different and odd, but criminal's lie all the time."

"But that's just a funny place to put them. If he needed the money like he said, why did he leave that much at home?"

"I agree. Puzzling. Go on to the next point."

"No one will verify his whereabouts in St. Louis." I picked up the autopsy report.

"Maybe because he wasn't there." He slurped again on his drink. "Any more?"

"Hmmm…" I was concentrating on the autopsy report.

"Mel?"

"I'm just reading the autopsy report."

"How did you get that?"

"Viking, the attorney, got it. Rich looked over all of the paperwork for him. I copied it."

"Mel…" Max's voice took on a warning tone.

"Don't go there, Max."

He sighed. "Did Rich find anything?"

"Nope." I quickly read the report. Most of it was in medical terms that I didn't understand. A small item caught my eye. "Hmmm."

"What?"

"Oh, just a small foot note in the autopsy report. It seems Ruth Meddleson had an STD when she died."

"So?"

"She's over sixty."

Max laughed. "Mel, older people have sex too, you know."

I grimaced. I was back to thinking of my grandmother doing it. "Don't even go there, Max. I don't need these kinds of images in my mind."

Max laughed harder.

"But… Hmmm…"

"Now what?"

"Well, an old lady neighbor said Ruth wanted a medical book to explain some terms. I wonder if it had anything..." I drifted off. *How could I find out if she knew she had an STD? More importantly, why did it matter?*

"Where are you going with this?"

"I don't know. Probably nowhere."

I heard him sigh. "Any other loose ends?"

"Not really. Not yet." I glanced up at the clock. I needed to get going to Mom and Dad's.

"But you'll find them?"

"If I look hard enough. I know Simon is innocent." I stacked all the reports back up. "I hate to cut this short but I'm due at Mom's for supper."

There was a long pause. "Just be careful, Mel."

CHAPTER 9

"Have more potatoes, Mel," Mom said as she plopped a spoonful on my plate.

I looked at Dad and rolled my eyes. "I said was I full."

Mom shook her head at me as she added more peas to my plate as well. "You're too thin. You need to eat more. You haven't gained back your weight from the accident."

"You know I was trying to lose weight before the accident." I gave Dad a 'save me' look.

Mom shook her head. "You still look sick." She smiled at me. "I want you to come over at least once a week for a meal-"

"Dot," Dad intoned softly and flashed a look at her when she turned her attention to him.

"Or maybe every other week," Mom finished without missing a beat.

I sighed and pushed the new food around on my plate.

"You seem sad tonight, Mel," Dad said.

I shrugged. "I talked with Max right before I came here."

Dad's eyes lightened. He liked Max.

"Max?" Mom asked. "Oh, that police officer that went back to California." She scraped the rest of the mashed potatoes toward one side of the bowl in preparation of putting it away.

"He said something that reminded me… of Robbie."

Dad's eyes softened as I looked at him.

Mom nodded. "I spoke with Father Joe at church about your situation…"

I rolled my eyes at Dad who sighed and cocked his head in defeat.

"… He thinks that you should join the adult meeting this Thursday on depression. I agree with him. Or even the Widow's Group that meets on…"

Like a thunderclap, my anger hit the explode stage. Knowing that I couldn't come unglued in front of them, I stood so quickly that I knocked the chair over. "Thanks for the meal, Mom." I headed for the door.

"Too far, Dot," Dad said as he followed me out the door. "Mel, wait."

I was already half way down the sidewalk to the parking lot on the alley. They owned three big lots. A three car garage sat on the alley with a four car parking lot next to it. I slowed but didn't stop.

"Mel!"

I stopped at the Jeep and waited. My breath came in gasps, my heart thundered in my ears, my fists clenched. *How dare she!*

"Calm down before you drive." His voice was the calm breeze that I needed.

He was right. I took a deep breath that dissipated most of the anger. Most of it. I turned around to face him. "She's driving me insane."

Dad gave me a half hearted grin. "Me too. She's constantly calling everyone asking about you."

"Everyone?"

"Yeah, especially Rich and Mitch." He leaned on the side of my Jeep Wrangler.

I joined him.

"She even called Teresa when she found out that you had talked to her last week."

"Why?" I should just give up and let Mom smother me. That's what she wanted to do.

"She thinks that you're not handling things right…"

I opened my mouth to speak but he continued.

"I know, I know. You're just grieving differently. She doesn't get that." Dad patted my arm. "How are you doing, Sweetie?"

I closed my mouth and sighed. "Fine. I have my moments, like this evening talking with Max, but overall I'm fine."

"Something is bothering you though. I can tell and so can Dot." He held up his hands in surrender to me. "I'm not saying that you have to tell me."

I nodded in thanks.

"But we're right, right?"

"I have… issues with… some things. Yes."

"Can we help at all?"

"No." I looked past the yard to the big mansion across the street from my parent's house. The trees, and they had plenty of them, always seemed peaceful to me. "I need- I have- I can't talk about it."

Dad nodded. "The accident. We never heard the full story. Is it concerning that?"

I didn't answer right away but stuck my hands in my pockets. I couldn't talk. I really couldn't. My lawyer had advised me to talk to no one. Not even family.

"Mel?"

I stood up off the Jeep and looked Dad in the eyes. "Thanks for the meal. Tell Mom I'm fine. And, to stop smothering."

Dad stared into my eyes, then I saw a look of understanding enter his blue eyes. "When you can…" He stopped, then gave me a kiss on the cheek. "Time. Take all the time you need, Sweetie."

When I got home, I paced the floor. Nothing I tried settled me. I thought about going downstairs to the bar and grabbing a beer. If nothing else, it would dull the jitters.

I wanted to tell someone. I glanced at the clock. *Should I call Jason Landry in Maryland?* As my lawyer, Craig's partner, I could talk with him freely. I shook my head. Too late at night, Maryland time, and I would feel weird calling him out of the blue. If I couldn't talk to family, I certainly couldn't talk to Beth or any of my other friends. But instinctively I knew I needed to talk to someone.

Someone who would listen and not judge.

I grabbed the portable phone and headed to the living room. Quickly before I lost my nerve, I dialed a number.

"Twice in one night. I'm honored." Max's smooth voice purred at me over the phone.

"Busy? Hope I'm not interrupting anything."

"Not at all. What's up?"

I hesitated. I shouldn't have called. "Nothing."

Max laughed. "I know so little about you, but I do know that 'nothing' is never what's up."

"I need a friend."

There was a pause on the line. "I'm honored you thought of me." He voice was soft. "Something's bothering you, uh?"

Tears formed in my eyes.

"You said you were having a meal… Ah, your mom uh?"

"Yeah. She's smothering again. But…."

"But? Something else?"

"I can't talk about it."

"How can I be a friend if you won't tell me what's bothering you?" he asked, his voice still quiet. "Okay…" I could now hear a smile in his voice. "Let's play Twenty Questions. Does it concern your family?"

I chuckled. "How did you know this was one of my favorite games as a kid?"

"You got your snooping sneak streak from somewhere. Now answer my first question."

"Yes."

"Okay. If tonight played a role, the smothering mom and all, this is about your husband and son."

I hesitated.

"Mel?"

I needed to side step this game. I shouldn't have started it in the first place. "That wasn't a question."

"Why can you bend the rules sometimes..." He sighed. "Is this about Craig and Robbie?"

I sniffled back the tears.

"Mel?"

"I don't want to play anymore."

"Aha, now I understand. There's something that you can't tell them, but you want to tell someone."

"I'm not playing and that wasn't even a question if I was playing." I sniffled again.

"The accident."

I didn't answer. Tears collecting in the corner of my eyes.

"Your lawyer told you not to talk."

I still didn't answer. Now the tears deepened, threatening to fall.

"Something to do with the lawsuit dealing with their deaths?"

I let the silence drag out. A swipe kept the tears contained, barely.

"So, have I helped?"

I sniffled then it abruptly turned into a laugh.

"Apparently I did." I could hear the smile in his voice. I held my side as I laughed. I knew he had to think I was a totally crazy moron, but all of the tension was gone. All the jitters fled. I knew I sounded insane, one minute almost crying and the next laughing almost uncontrollably, but I couldn't go any further.

He chuckled over the phone. "Feel better?"

"Much. You got it all wrong, but thanks anyway."

"I read people very well. And Tiger, I'm know I'm not wrong."

***

I stopped by Earl Boden's place the next day. He was in the garden doing something to his flowers. As I walked up to him, I heard him muttering to himself. With a smile, I cleared my throat. "Hi, Mr. Boden."

He jumped and looked at me in surprise. Scruffy jumped too and came running from his place on the back porch. He growled once and tried to stare menacingly at me. Shaking as he did so.

"Sorry to scare you, Mr. Boden, Scruffy. Mr. Viking mentioned the other day that you were watching after the Meddleson house until the whole thing was settled. I was wondering if I could take a look around the house?" I bent down and let Scruffy sniff my hand. Finally the little dog let me pet him. His tail even wagged. Grudgingly.

"What for?"

I shrugged, standing back up. "Just to get a feel for the crime scene." In reality, I wanted to check out her medicine cabinet. Maybe get a look at her answering machine or caller ID, hoping the cops hadn't taken everything. At the very least, I wanted to just poke around. Curiosity. Insatiable curiosity.

"I'm busy right now." Boden held up his hands. He was covered in dirt to his elbows.

"Not a problem. I can come back later or, since I work for Simon, could I just borrow the keys and bring them back?"

Boden frowned. "Are you looking for something specific?"

I hesitated. "Not really. Viking thought that since I was a woman..." I shrugged letting him finish the statement anyway he wanted. This particular statement left unfinished usually works wonders, especially on men.

"Well..." Boden considered hard. "I suppose I could let you, since you work for Simon's attorney. I'll let you go over there, but I'll be there in a few minutes after I clean up. Not that I don't trust you, but-"

"You don't trust me." I smiled. "I understand, Mr. Boden. If you want, I could wait for you."

Almost embarrassed, he shook his head. "No. I'll be along in a while. Go ahead. Ruth's keys are on the fourth key hook from the end. There's a dog tag attached to them."

I headed in and retrieved them. "By the way, Mr. Boden, you wouldn't by any chance have a picture of Winnie, would you?"

"Maybe. Why?"

"He's missing. Simon's worried. I was hoping to show it around. You know, see if anyone has seen him."

Boden frowned. "I'll see if I can find one."

"Thanks. I'll wait for you at the house if I finish before you get there." With a good-bye pat for Scruffy, I headed away. Over my shoulder I saw Boden watch me until I started to pull away from the curb. Then he hurried inside.

***

The interior of Ruth Meddleson's house had a strange smell. I stood just inside the living room scanning the house. The blood stain was still in the carpet. I could see smudges of stuff that looked like dust on various items in the room, most likely fingerprint dust. Part of the blood stained carpet had been cut away, taken by the police. The feeling in the house was almost oppressive. It was so silent.

I left the main door open to let in some fresh air through the screen. As I walked around the room, I noted where things were, wondering what had been moved by the police and what had been where for the actual murder. I knew from experience that this room had been combed and search in depth. The Quincy Police were thorough. And Tom Hawkings, the lead detective and Rich's best friend, was even more so.

The kitchen was in a similar condition. Clean and tidy except where the police had obviously been working. I slowly inspected the entire kitchen without touching anything. With a frown, I moved over to the sink and looked down. The police had removed one of the drain traps. This must have been the place where the murderer had cleaned up.

The answering machine in the kitchen was an older one and both tapes were missing. No caller ID. I picked up the phone and hit the redial.

It was answered on the first ring. "Hello?"

I sucked in a breath, my brain spun into overdrive instantly. "Uh, Mr. Boden… I was wondering if you wanted me to open the windows in here. It's sort of smelly." I swallowed, hoping it didn't sound too made up on the spot. Boden was the last person Ruth had called before she had died. *Why?*

"Sure. I was going to open them up again tonight. Go ahead."

"Thanks, Mr. Boden." I hung up, wondering about the call. The police hadn't known that, as far as I could tell. Interesting, but it probably meant nothing. After all, he was a good neighbor.

I moved down the hall into the downstairs bathroom. The medicine cabinet was open. Apparently the police had searched it too. Disappointed, I heading upstairs to look at Simon's room.

What a mess. Clothes on the floor. Plates encrusted with old, moldy food. Glasses everywhere. It looked more like a teenager's room than a grown man's room. There were papers everywhere. Again, the police had obviously searched this room.

The second bedroom was messy too. *Maybe a junk room.* There were boxes piled up and miscellaneous items literally thrown around the room. I poked here and there. One box had unmarked videos. Another had lingerie in it. I smiled, thinking back to Max's laugh. Then I shook myself. I didn't want to be thinking about old people doing it.

I shut the boxes and moved into what was Ruth's bedroom. My eyes immediately went to the small dog bed in the corner, but it didn't appear to have been used much. The bed covers were messed up. I guess Ruth didn't make beds either. And all over the bed sheets was dog hair. Small brown and white hairs. Ruth obviously let Winnie sleep with her in bed.

The closet showed some expensive dress clothes, along with more 'normal' clothes, jeans and less dressy shirts. There was even a floor length gown in there. Lots of shoes too. I stepped back and quickly did a count. *At least fifty pairs. Why would an older lady want that many long spiky heels and stiletto type boots?*

I hated heels. I always felt like I was on stilts and about to fall. I rifled through the clothes again. Yes, several designer dresses and suits.

I spied a small bag, like a carry-on bag, on the shelf in the closet. When I opened it, I gasped. A blond wig and a cheerleaders outfit! Quickly, I replaced it before I let my thoughts take me somewhere I didn't want them going.

Another bag was tucked behind that. In this one was a red wig with a red bustier, thigh-high fishnet nylons and a fake leopard skin skirt. I shuttered as I tossed it back onto the shelf. The last bag, which was a lot heavier, I almost didn't open. I had seen more than enough, but curiosity won out. As always.

This one contained a chain, handcuffs, a small leather outfit, a paddle, padded restrains of some sort, a ball gag and a whip. This bag I threw back up on the shelf as fast as possible.

"Oh man, I didn't need to see that. Yuck!" I said out loud. "Think about the dog. Focus on the dog." I chanted as I moved away from the closet.

Her dresser drawers revealed another surprise. More lingerie. The woman must have really like her underclothes. Some rather risqué. *No, stop thinking like that.* I didn't want to imagine her…

I closed the drawer quickly. Ugh!

Her bathroom didn't cough up any meds either. I sighed. If the police took any medicines it would have been listed on the reports. I would need to read them in more depth tonight.

I expeditiously went through her trashcans in the room. If the guys had taught me anything, it was that trash was a gold mine, but not in this case.

I moved to her bed again and checked out the night stand. A paperback mystery novel was laid face down, opened.

Lastly, I lifted up the mattress. I knew it was a cliché to think that someone might actually hide something of importance there. And it proved right. Nothing. As an afterthought, I looked under the bed. The dust ruffle was hiding huge dust bunnies that she had been breeding under the bed.

I sneezed. As I started to sneeze again, I saw something move, besides the bunnies. Part of the box spring dust covering was torn away and had blown in my sneeze. Amidst another sneeze I reached inside the hole and felt around. My hand made contact with a small book of some sort.

I sat on the floor, sneezed again, then shook my hand because the book had picked up dust on the trip from under the bed. It was a little spiral notebook.

I opened it.

The door banged closed on the lower floor. Quickly, I stood and shoved the notebook into my pocket. With a last glance, I headed out. I met Mr. Boden on the stairs.

"Find anything?"

I rubbed my nose. "Just a brace of rabbits." I smiled at Boden's puzzled expression. "Under the bed."

Boden's look changed to relief, then he chuckled. "Ruth wasn't one to vacuum much."

We headed to the kitchen. "What's going to happen to the house, Mr. Boden?"

"Mr. Viking says that it all depends on the outcome of Simon's trial. If he's convicted, it'll be sold. I assume Simon is using the house as collateral to pay his attorney. If Simon is acquitted for some reason… Well, I guess he'll still have to sell to pay his attorney." Boden looked around the kitchen. He picked up a rag and wetted it in the downstairs bathroom, then wiped the counters.

"I guess Simon will inherit all of Ruth's money, since he's the only heir," I said as I watched him clean.

Boden's head snapped to look at me. "I thought..." He swiped at the cabinet door where it looked like the police had dusted for prints. "I thought he already had taken all of her money?"

"I don't think so. I think Viking mentioned something about some money in another account." I watched as Boden continued to clean. It seemed like a reflex for him.

"Hmmm. Even if he goes to prison?"

"That's my understanding."

Boden shook his head. "Incredible. He does all this and still gets away with her money."

I noticed a pile of mail on the table. I sat down and looked through it.

"I forgot to pick up the mail the past couple of days," Boden said watching me. "I guess I need to take it all to Mr. Viking so that he can make sure the bills get paid or something."

I paged through them rather quickly but two caught my eye. One was a letter from St. Louis. It looked like a business letter. The company name on the logo was Entertainment Extravaganza. The other was from a clinic also in St. Louis. I didn't stop to look at them though, I could see Boden watching me out of the corner of my eye. I laid the pile back on the table and sighed.

"What are you looking for? Maybe I can help?"

"Well..." I sighed again for effect. "I was hoping to find something that maybe the police didn't."

"Like?"

"I don't know." I looked around the kitchen, trying to think of a way to change the subject. *The dog.* "Did Ruth let Winnie outside by himself?"

"Occasionally."

I stood up. "Maybe there's a hole in the fence or something. Maybe he crawled out and got away."

"Possible," Boden said turning around to look out the window. "Winnie thinks he's big, only he's stuck in a small dog body. Ferocious little dog. If something made him mad, he might go after it. Maybe over by the corner. Ruth said one time she had cats coming in that way. That was before she got Winnie."

I snagged the two letters and stuffed them under my shirt in back. "Can you show me where?"

"Sure." Boden folded the dishcloth and laid it on the counter.

I followed him out the door. As he folded the washcloth, I shoved the envelopes further down the back of my pants. I smoothed the shirt back into place as we exited the house.

The back yard was a mess. The grass obviously hadn't been cut in a while. Of course, most of the 'grass' were weeds anyway. There was a broken chair under a tree and trash lying in places.

Boden squatted at the back fence. "Looks like Simon must've fixed the hole." He pointed to the wooden patch near the ground.

I turned and looked at the whole yard.

A voice called over the fence, "Hello, Earl."

Boden stood up. "Hello, Frank. This is Mel Addison. She's working for Viking, Simon's attorney."

Mr. Allen's gaze came back to me. "So I've heard. You were the one the other day knocking on our door." The tone wasn't friendly.

"Yes I was, Mr. Allen." I hesitated, maybe if I try a new tactic. "Now I'm looking for Winnie. Have you seen him since the murder?" Most people have a soft spot for pets, especially cute little ones.

Allen's face changed to one of understanding. "No, can't say that I have. Funny that. No. Not since, well, since Ruth put him out the night she was killed. Winnie was barking at Jumper."

"Jumper?" I asked moving closer to the fence.

Mr. Allen smiled. "Our name for the resident squirrel. Jumper. He loves to jump from the fence onto Mary's bird feeder. Little rascal. No matter what we do the little guy always finds a way to get the corn and seeds in the bird feed." Mr. Allen shook his head in amusement. "He keeps us on our toes."

"And Winnie was barking at him that night?"

Allen nodded.

"How late?"

He thought about it. "The sun was setting so, oh, around maybe seven o'clock or so."

"Hmm," I said absentmindedly and looked around the back yard again. I turned back to see both men watching me. "Mr. Allen, if you see or hear anything about Winnie will you call me? I'm really worried about him."

He hesitated but nodded.

I handed him a card then Boden and I went back inside the house. "Did you find a picture of Winnie for me?"

Boden shook his head. "I can't find any at my place, but I'm sure Ruth has a couple here somewhere." He headed into the living room.

I followed.

After rummaging around in a drawer of a desk in the living room, Boden produced a picture. Winnie was well groomed. His hair was brushed and shined in the sun.

"Cute dog."

Boden stared at the floor. "Yeah."

"You said you thought that the police gave him to Ruth's niece in Canton?"

Boden glanced up.

"I called her. She doesn't have him. The police didn't even mention Winnie to her."

Boden shrugged. "Then Winnie was probably killed by Simon too." He shook his head. "I'm sure he didn't mean to hurt Winnie. I guess Winnie was an unintentional victim."

"Seems that way, but where is the body if Winnie is dead?"

We both stood there for several minutes in silence. I was looking around the room again. My eyes came to rest on the blood stain. I sighed. *Where should I go or do next?*

Suddenly a thought struck me. I hadn't seen Winnie's bowls in the kitchen. I moved back to the kitchen. My movement must have scared Boden because he jumped.

"Where did Ruth feed Winnie?"

"What?" Boden had followed me into the kitchen.

"There are no dog bowls."

Boden looked around as though for the first time at the kitchen. "Yeah. You're right."

"Odd." I took one more look around the kitchen. *Definitely odd.* "Well, thanks for letting me look here, Mr. Boden."

"Sure." He took the keys from my hands.

After we locked up, I offered him a ride home.

"Thanks. I'll walk."

I climbed in the Jeep.

"Mel." He stopped me from pulling away. "Are you still coming over to Stella's house for the card game on Friday?"

"Do you still want to get beat, Mr. Boden?" I smiled.

He grinned back. "A bet?"

I nodded.

"Ten dollars to the winner."

"And what if Mrs. Beaverton wins?" I asked.

"Then we each give her a ten."

I chuckled. "You're on."

I drove away from the Meddleson house and stopped several blocks away to secure the notebook. I took a closer look at the letters but wanting to wait on opening them until I was comfortable at home. I decided to check in with Roma.

She wasn't home. I stopped before getting back into my Jeep and looked around. *If I were stalking someone, where would I watch her house from?* My eyes roamed her neighborhood. It was mixed residential and business. I spied a convenience store half a block away. It had pay phones. *Could he be calling from there?*

The small strip mall another block down would be too far away. The fast food business would be another place to sit and watch, especially since Roma's house didn't have an alley and she parked in the driveway on the side of her house.

My eyes panned over the neighbors' houses and one apartment building. It had four units, two on each level. There was lots of traffic, which didn't make our job easier.

I took a deep breath. Too many places to watch at the same time. My phone rang as I pulled away from the curb. "Hello?"

"Sorry I missed you the other night at the bar, Mel."

I grimaced. Bart Hessor. *How did he get my cell number?* "That's okay. I couldn't stick around."

"Busy tonight?"

"Actually, yeah."

"I heard that you and your brother were looking into the Meddleson murder."

"Yeah. Was."

"So I heard."

"How?"

"Let's just say I have snitches all over the place."

"Including in the Adams County Jail?"

Bart laughed. "Among others."

"Why do you mention it?"

"I'm interested in you, Mel. I told you that before. Maybe I can help you."

"How?"

"Simon said he was at Rascals."

How did he know this stuff? I frowned. "Yeah."

"I know some people down in St. Louis-"

"I bet you do."

"Now, do you want my help or not?"

I hesitated. "Maybe."

"Good." I could hear the grin in his voice. He knew he had me over a barrel. "Friday. I'll go down there with you and see if we can't scare up Punky."

"I'm busy Friday."

"Saturday then. It's busier that day anyway," Bart said with a satisfied tone.

"I'll think about it and get back to you."

"Do that." He hung up.

I cursed under my breath. He was using his connections to get me in his debt. Then he would try and use that to get me into a compromising situation.

But, I had no other choice.

CHAPTER 10

That night I read the little notebook I had taken from under Ruth's bed. It only had names and phone numbers. Some of the numbers had no names. A couple had stars by them. One had a smiley face. Two were highlighted in pink.

Tomorrow, I would run the names and numbers through the data bases to see what they brought up. The reverse directory ought to get me addresses and names for the ones with numbers only.

The letter from Entertainment Extravaganza had more names and numbers. Hand written on the bottom was a note.

'You had better make these appointments.'

I glanced at the clock but it was too late to try the numbers listed in the letterhead to see what this business was. Again, I set it aside for tomorrow.

The clinic note was a form letter. It said that the results were in and included a confidential number. Jb4527r3364y24. Then a phone number. Further down the letter it stated the call would not be monitored and the results would only be released to a doctor with the patient's written permission.

I picked up the portable phone as it rang.

"He's calling me," Roma's voice sounded scared.

"Did he actually leave a message?"

"Yeah."

"Tell me what he said."

"He said that he was back. That's all it said. Oh Mel, I'm so scared." She sniffled. "I just got back in the house. The phone rang right away. He must have been following me."

"Okay. Are the doors locked?"

"Yeah."

"Let me call Rich and find out what he wants you to do. One of us will be by in a few minutes. Don't open the door unless you hear our voices."

"Okay. Thank you, Mel."

"Sit tight." I hung up and speed dialed Rich's home phone number. He wasn't home. He didn't answer his cell either. I cursed under my breath and dialed John's cell.

"Yeah?"

"Roma just called me…." I detailed for John the conversation.

"Okay. I'm close by her house. Call her back. Tell her I'll stop by and check out the area. I won't actually come to her house though." John paused. "Is she okay?"

"Panicked, but okay."

"Tell her to stay calm. He wants to terrorize her. I'll find a place to watch her house for awhile."

"Sure thing. Thanks, John."

I dialed Roma back. I got her answering machine. "Roma, it's Mel…"

"Mel!" Roma picked it up in a hurry.

I relayed the conversation with John to her. "In the morning, I'll talk to Rich. Save the tape, Roma. Don't tape over it."

"I know." She sighed. "I feel at least a little better." She hesitated. "Is John any good at what he does? I mean, he was so quiet in the meeting."

"John used to be a Special Forces Ranger in the Army. He's good."

"Good."

"Call at any time."

"Thanks."

I hung up shaking my head. I couldn't imagine what it must feel like to have someone watching my every move. *Weird.* The phone rang again in my hand. "Hello?"

"Hey, Tiger."

"Max, I thought you were working today."

"I am. Pulled surveillance again. I'm bored out of my skull."

"Should you be talking to me? Aren't you supposed to be keeping your mind on the person?"

Max laughed. "He's eating in a restaurant. I can see him through the window. He's such a pig." He paused. "Man, now I'm hungry."

I chuckled.

"Busy for a few minutes?"

"Nope."

"How's the search for the little Shih Tzu going?"

"Still missing." I hesitated. "Max, I got a question for you."

"Okay."

"If you have a source of information that you really don't want to use… I mean how ethical is it to use this source, knowing that you're not going to follow through on what the source wants in return?"

74

Max chuckled. "Mel, you're being vague again. Who's the source and what does he want?"

"A guy and a date."

There was no answer on the other line.

"Max?"

"Yeah. I can't make that decision for you. It's up to your conscience. How important is this information and is it worth putting your feelings on the line?"

I sighed. "Yeah."

"Personally, I don't want you to go out with any-" Max interrupted himself. "Gotta go, my suspect's on the move. Don't do anything that you'll regret. That's my best advice. I don't want you going- Gotta go."

"See ya." I hung the phone. With a frown, I dialed the number on the clinic paper.

It was an automated system and I followed the directions. After putting in the confidential number, the program told me it was accessing the information.

"The test was positive. The HIV virus is confirmed. If you wish to have this information forwarded to your doctor, please press number one. If you would like to talk to a counselor, please press two..."

I hung up the phone. *Ruth's name was on the envelope, but was Ruth HIV positive or Simon?*

***

Rich, John and I sat discussing the Roma situation the next morning. John had sat near her house for two hours but Devon didn't appear. Rich put forth the idea that Devon could have been calling from anywhere, just because he called didn't necessarily mean he was in Quincy.

It was decided to have Roma continued to record his calls, at the same time each of us would take turns driving by her house at odd times. I called Roma and told her that she should report to us the next time he was on the phone. Hopefully, we could be in the area when he called. She gave us her cell phone number, and she would use it until he found out about it.

I sat for the rest of the morning doing more employee checks. When I finished with those, I began running the names from Ruth Meddleson's little notebook. Most of them came up nonexistent or they weren't from our area code. I frowned. Where could they be from? I tried the St. Louis area code, but it showed that that was not right either. Three were from in town, all highlighted in pink.

One was a Ralph Hegstrom. I ran his name through the usual data bases and found out he was the owner of a local mail box store. The second was to a guy by the name of Hilton Craser. His name brought up nothing important in the data bases. He worked for a local tree trimming business. The last name was listed as the office number of a church. *Did Ruth go to church?* None of the neighbors mentioned anything like that.

I decided to drive past the church and speak with someone this afternoon.

I was just dialing the number for the business in St. Louis when Pam announced that I had a call. I switched lines, "Hello?"

"Ms. Addison?"

"Yes. Who is this?"

"Frank Allen. I, uh… I spoke with Mary last night and she… She said that she was worried about little Winnie too."

"Yes?"

"Uh… She got up late that night and went to the kitchen to get a drink. Our kitchen is right off the back porch facing the backyard. Anyway, she thought she heard Winnie whimpering or crying late that night."

"The night Ruth Meddleson was killed?"

"Yes. She thinks so."

"Whimpering?" My mind flashed to the garbage bag that I had gone through. *Was the matted hair Winnie's? Had he been hurt? And was that blood on the t-shirt Ruth's, as everyone had thought or was it Winnie's?*

"Mary thought it odd that he went on for so long before it stopped. Ruth never let Winnie whimper."

"Hmmm."

"She also said it sounded like he yelped once before the whining stopped. She said it was late, but didn't know when. She gets up several times a night to, well, do her business."

"Okay." I frowned. "This doesn't sound good for Winnie."

"Yes."

"Mr. Allen, again, if you see Winnie please call me."

"Sure."

"Thanks for the call Mr. Allen."

"Uh… Will you call us if you find Winnie?"

"I will. Out of curiosity, why?"

"Well, now that we've been thinking about it, when Simon goes to prison, Winnie will have nowhere to go. If you find him, and no one wants him, I'm sure Earl will want him but if not, he can have a home with us."

I smiled. "I will."

"Thank you, Ms. Addison. And, uh, sorry about how we didn't help-"

I interrupted him. "It's perfectly understandable, Mr. Allen. I have no hard feelings."

"Good."

I hung up with a smile. So, Winnie was alive after Ruth was dead. Whoever killed Ruth then took care of the little mutt. This did not look good for Winnie. And now I would have to re-canvas the local vets and animal hospitals for a wounded dog, not just a stray.

Again I was dialing the number for Entertainment Extravaganza when John called for me from his office. I sighed softly, set the phone back down and headed his way. "Yeah?"

"Sit. I need some help with a case. I'm working on a domestic case and I need help with surveillance and... womanly help."

"Womanly help?" I smiled. "Okay. When and where?"

John smiled back. "I need you to work with the lady at her job. Talk to her."

I frowned. "Where?"

"Home Town Pizzeria."

"A waitress?!"

John almost chuckled. "You're a good waitress."

I made a sour face. "How are you going to get me a job there?"

"I know the manager. He's already agreed to put you on the payroll, in name only, until we finish this. They won't be paying you, but you do get to keep any tips."

"Bonus." It was heavy with sarcasm.

John chuckled. "Will you do it?"

I shrugged. "When does my shift start?"

"Tonight. Tony, the manager, is coming in a few minutes to meet you and tell you what you'll need to know."

"For how long?" I didn't really want this to interfere with the Friday night card game. I wanted to quiz Mrs. Beaverton some more.

John shrugged. "Until we find out who she's cheating with. Tony's putting you one the same shift as Carla Rosen."

"That's the lady?"

"Yep. Her husband suspects she's cheating on him."

"Is she?"

"Yeah, I think so. I need some sort of proof, though."

"And my job? Besides wearing down my shoes?"

John smiled again. "See if you can get her to talk about him or where or anything."

"Sounds like you're grasping at straws."

"In a nut shell."

***

I rang the bell of the church office and waited. I didn't have a lot of time to spend, I had to be at my 'new job' in an hour.

The door opened to reveal a middle aged man. He was clean shaven and had his glasses in his hand. The brown hair was tousled and his eyes looked me up and down. "May I help you?"

"Maybe. I'm not sure." I smiled.

He smiled back. "You seem troubled. Come in." He motioned me into the room and closed the door. He pointed to what was obviously a sitting room in the office area. It was a small, separate room and contained two chairs and a small couch.

"What can I do for you?"

After sitting, I squirmed once. I had always hated talking with my parish priest and this seemed too much like a confessional. I swallowed. "I'm not really sure how to ask or what to ask."

His smile was sympathetic. "First off, my name is Gordon Grace. I'm the pastor here. What's your name?"

"Mel Addison. And this isn't what you're thinking."

"What am I thinking, Ms. Addison?" His voice had taken on that priestly 'I understand you have problems' voice.

"Mel. Please call me Mel." I took a breath. "I work for Security Investigations and the number of this office showed up in relation to an investigation. I was wondering if you could enlighten me about why this number was where it was?"

He frowned. His eyes got wary.

"The number to the office here was found in a little book of Ruth Meddleson's."

His eyes darkened and he stiffened.

"Did you know her? Does she attend church here?"

He hesitated. Standing, he quickly shut the door then sat back down. "What's this in relationship too?"

"I'm investigating the murder of Ruth Meddleson for Simon, her son, and his attorney." *Well okay, this was not good. Here I was in the house of God, lying through my teeth to a man of God. I was going to hell on the next train.*

"And this notebook?"

"It was found in Ruth's house. I'm trying to track down the numbers in the book." I paused, as Reverend Grace shifted in his chair. He put his glasses on the end table and then tugged at his shirt sleeve. "It's merely for background on Ruth and her life. Simon says he's innocent. We're trying to keep him from getting the death penalty. To that end, we're desperately trying to find out who really killed Ruth." I was hoping that like most priests and ministers I had met, he was against the death penalty. *That train I was on, was the express train, making no stops on its fiery trip to hell.*

He looked off to the side of me then looked me in the eyes. "And if I reveal to you why, what will be done with the information?"

"It depends on what the information is. Most likely it'll never even be written up in my report. As I said, it's just background." *The train was already on fire, I could feel the flames licking at my heels.*

Gordon rubbed his face. "I have had many a conversation with God about this."

This has to be revealing.

"I'm ashamed, but if this information ever got out, it would break up my family and destroy my life. Yet, I'm guilty of the worst of sins." He bowed his head.

My eyes widened. Whatever this was, it had been eating at him for awhile now. "Reverend Grace..."

"I don't deserve the title anymore. Call me Gordon."

"Gordon, I promise that the information won't leave my lips. I only want to help save, Simon. Can you understand that?" *The hair on my legs started smoking.*

"I do. And I need to take responsibility for my actions." Gordon looked up. "Ruth and I had a sexual encounter."

I almost gasped out loud. Ruth was in her mid sixties, this man couldn't have been more than forty-five. I tried to marshal my face into neutrality.

"Yes, I know." Gordon nodded. "I have always had a soft spot for older woman. Even in my youth, the older woman was a heavy temptation that I strove hard to resist. I... I saw Ruth once. Lust took over. I betrayed my vows to my wife. The devil was strong."

I didn't know what to say. This was not at all what I was expecting.

Gordon clenched his hands, then began wringing them. Now that the gate had been opened, it seemed he wanted to talk about it. "I saw her at a convention in St. Louis. I struck up a conversation with her. When she found out I was soon heading here to Quincy, she... uh, well, we got more friendly. One thing led to another. When I moved here, she came by a couple of times. My wife was gone both of those times. I'm deeply ashamed of my actions."

"How long ago was this?"

"She could tell how distraught it was making me, I think. Ruth was a good woman. I was extremely saddened when I heard she had died, although it did cause a weight to be lifted from my shoulders. My temptation was gone." He glanced up. "Not that it was Ruth's fault. No. I was the one who sinned. I'm responsible for my actions. It was wrong. So terribly wrong."

"How long ago was this?" I tried again.

"She was a good... What?" He finally looked at me. "Oh, it's been awhile now. Maybe six months since I last saw her."

His name had been about mid-notebook. The two others in pink were later in the book. "Can you tell me anything about her, Gordon?"

"She was really a good listener. I guess that is a stereotype but it was really true in her case." He almost blushed. "She was gentle and understanding. I've-I've had problems with- She was very understanding. Yes, may her soul rest in peace." He touched his breast. Looking at me, I could tell he was done talking.

I stood and handed him a business card. "If you think of anything else, Gordon, please give me a call."

His eyes glanced at the card then came to rest on my face.

"I won't reveal anything to anyone. If you want to, well, that's up to you and your conscience." I smiled and patted him on the shoulder. "Thank you for being candid with me."

"No." He stood quickly. "No, thank you for helping me. I feel as though a burden has been partially lifted."

We shook hands.

In the car, I shuddered. *Concentrate on the dog. Think about poor Winnie.* I did not want to go down this path. Not at all.

***

The computer was slow the next morning as I waited for it to cough up the list of veterinarians from the Hannibal, Missouri phone book. I had called all of the vets in the Quincy area to see if anyone had brought in a stray dog. No such luck. I'd try all of the surrounding towns, just in case.

Rich appeared at my doorway.

"Yeah?"

His face was hard and his blue eyes were flashing anger. He held up some phone messages. "These came in late yesterday and early this morning."

I held out my hand for them.

Rich didn't move. "Holden Street Pet Vet. Ruthies's Cat and Dog Clinic. Maude Veterinarian Hospital. Ellis Small Animal Medical Clinic."

I swallowed.

"We're off of the case, Mel. Off. As in stop looking into this."

"I get it. I was just checking on the-"

"Then I get a call early this morning before Pam came in." He tossed the pile in front of me. "Entertainment Extravaganza."

I gathered the pile before looking at him. He was steaming mad.

"I'm not going to ask who or what they are. It's a St. Louis phone number. The man was real vague why he was returning your phone call." The blue eyes of my brother were iceberg cold. "This is your last warning. We are off the case. Leave it alone. Let the dog go."

"But-"

"No buts, Mel. If you continue to follow up on this, I'll fire you. And when the family comes down on me for it, I'll tell them exactly what went on. Do I make myself clear, *little sister*?"

I swallowed again. All I could do was nod. I had only seen him this mad once before and I did not want a repeat of that time. I'd been a teen, he was already a police officer, and he had taken me out to the garage to 'talk' to me about one of my many stupid teenage stunts. He had literally laid down the law.

"Good." Rich spun on his heel and left.

I placed the pile of messages in front of me and stared at them. My eyes lifted to the doorway. I hit the enter button, sending the list of Hannibal veterinarians to the printer.

CHAPTER 11

Before showing up for 'work' again, at the pizzeria, I stopped by the Mail Box Place. Ralph Hegstrom, the owner, was in but I had to wait ten minutes to talk with him in private. Finally, the business was empty.

"Yes?"

I introduced myself and the reason that I was there.

His eyes hardened. He immediately adopted a belligerent tone. "I don't know what you're talking about."

"As I said, you're phone number is listed in her book. I'm merely asking, confidentially, how you know her and why your number is in her book?"

"Get out." Hegstrom pointed to the door. "Get out. NOW!"

I stood my ground for a few seconds then departed. The last thing I needed was to have to explain to the police or worse, Rich, why I was arrested for harassment.

The problem of Ruth continued to bug me all the while I worked at the pizzeria. The restaurant was actually a pretty decent job.

There were three of us scheduled that night until ten. It was just after seven and the main dinner rush was over. I sighed as I rubbed my one shoe with the other. Even my favorite, most comfortable tennis shoes were not helping my feet tonight.

"Hey, Mel," Carla said as she moved in close. "A guy seated at table four in my area just gave me a ten to let you wait on him."

I sighed. "Man! I was getting ready to take a half hour break and eat. I'm starving."

Carla smiled and cocked her head in the table's direction. "He's gorgeous."

I turned with a slight frown on my face to the table in question. Sitting at the table was Max Bauer. His smile lit up the room like a spot light. He winked. I smiled back with a shake of my head.

"Do you want him?"

"Yeah. Order me a Jeff's special. Just let me know when it's up." I grabbed some chips and salsa that we gave everyone for free and headed to the table. "Lucky for you Bauer, I was going on break."

Max laughed. "Good. Have you eaten?"

"I already ordered a pizza for us. What do you want to drink?"

After retrieving the drinks, I sat opposite him in the booth. "What brings you back to Quincy?"

"I decided since you wouldn't come out to see me, I'd come here." Max lifted his eyebrows. "I traded a day off for, well, let's just say, I'm going to be a slave to a fellow detective for the next two weeks, taking his on call."

I chuckled.

Max looked around the restaurant. "Since you didn't answer your phone, I tracked down Rich. He said you were here, 'working undercover'." There was a glint in his eyes.

"Yeah." I glanced around. Carla was busy with another table so I pointed her out. "Carla's the one I'm watching. She's having an affair, I did confirm that. I snuck a peek at one of her text messages, sex talk then a question about tonight. But with whom and where? Who knows."

"Rich said this was John's case."

"Yeah. Being the peon…"

Max chuckled.

"So, how long are you here?"

"Day and a half. I leave from St. Louis late Thursday night. I'll need to leave late that afternoon." Max took a drink while he stared into my eyes. "I'm sleeping on Steve Wettle's couch for the duration. When do you get off tonight?"

"Ten."

"Want to do something?" He quickly added, "As friends."

I gave him a smile. "Sure, I guess. As long as it doesn't involve walking."

The half hour flew by. Max was always fun to pal around with. I paid for the meal out of my tips and agreed to meet him at my place.

I headed back to the grind so Carla could have a half hour off. The place slowed considerably. I was wrapping up silverware when I ran out of napkins. After checking under the counter and not finding any, I frowned. "Millie, where do you keep the extra napkins?" I asked the other waitress as she put in another order.

"Uh, under the counter."

"I checked there. Out."

"Then you'll have to get some from the over stock closet. It's near the back door, through the kitchen," she said over her shoulder, grabbing some chips for a table.

"Thanks," I called to her as she hurried away. I glanced at my two tables that had customers but they appeared to be doing okay. So I headed through the kitchen with a nod at Hector who was flipping dough in the air.

As I neared the door, Hector called out, "Mel, wait!"

I looked back at him as I pulled open the door. He dropped the dough on the table with a thump, flour billowing out in a white cloud, as he hurried toward me. Hector was still saying something but I wasn't listening. I heard noises from inside the room. I stepped through the door just as he reached my side and pulled me back into the hall.

"Nothing in here…" Hector said but I knew better.

The grunts, groans and expulsions of breath were familiar sounds. I glanced over my shoulder to see Carla rocking on top of someone.

Hector shut the door, shaking his head. "Nothing happening here. Got it?"

"But-"

Hector glared at me. I decided to play the 'stupid girl'. "Look, Carla was-"

"Nothing. Forget what you saw." He crossed his arms trying to look stern.

"Who-"

Hector grabbed my arm and headed me into the kitchen. "Look, Carla is married. Don't wreck her marriage. She's got two kids. Okay?"

I stood my ground. "Stupid place to have an affair."

"Yeah, tell me about it." He sighed and picked up the dough, once more flipping it into the air. He had a look of disbelief on his face. "Couldn't go to their normal place. She thinks her husband is checking up on her. If you ask me, she's just asking for trouble. And D? How stupid is he, doing a married woman." He glanced at me as the dough flew up again. "You'll play along, right?"

"It's not my life." I looked back to the closest and almost grinned. "I still need napkins."

"I'll get them when D comes back to cook. Okay? We cool?"

"Sure." I glanced at my watch, heading back to the front counter. After checking on my tables, I hurried to the lobby to call John.

"Yeah?"

"You owe me."

"Yeah?"

"I just walked in on them. Back room here at the restaurant. The guy D, Derek Sanders, the cook."

John chuckled. "I'll call the husband right now."

"Do I have to finish out my shift here?"

"I'll ask Tony."

"Thanks." I was hoping not, I was tired.

"I heard Max Bauer was in town."

"Yeah. News travels fast around here."

"Thanks for the help, Mel."

"Sure. Does that mean I'm getting a raise?"

"You got your tips, didn't you?"

"Funny, John."

I made it home around nine. Tony thanked me for working so hard, and even offered me a job if I ever needed one. He had received three compliments about me in just two days of work. Thinking about how I had defied Rich by staying on the case, I might need to take him up on the offer, real soon.

After taking a shower, I called Roma on her cell phone. "Hi, Mel." There was a bright smile in her voice.

"Anything happening?"

"He's left three messages tonight. And, of course, they came after I got home, so I know he's following me. I haven't seen him yet."

"What's the tone of the messages? Is he still just saying he's back?"

"No." There was a sigh. "I called Rich earlier about his last one." She paused slightly. "Listen in on this next one, the answering machine just picked up. I turned off the ringer. I was getting sick of it. Listen." It sounded like she put the cell phone to the answering machine.

"Hello, Roma. When did you stop using Tide? I'm watching you," the male voice sneered at her.

"See what I mean, Mel. I went to the grocery store tonight. He was close enough to see what I bought."

"I'll tell Rich in the morning. Since Devon was specific about seeing you, maybe we can get a police report and push for an arrest warrant or, at the least, maybe contact his parole officer and get an agent's warrant to get him off the streets... if I understand the system. If you don't hear from me by ten, call the office." I turned at a knock on my door. Getting up as I spoke, I hurried to look out.

Max Bauer.

I opened the door and motioned him in. "So, sit tight, Roma. If you have any problems, call my cell. If it sounds like he's trying to break in or anything, call 911. My brother Mitch is a cop and he's working nights. He's generally in your area. I'll call him and have him keep a special eye out."

"Thanks." I heard her sniffle. "I- You guys are actually doing more than I'm paying you for. I appreciate you- tell your brother, Mitch, thanks."

"It's what we do." I smiled at Max as he sat at the counter. I reseated myself at my place quickly gathering the file on Simon's case and putting it away. "Remember Roma, call any of us. Okay?"

"Thanks."

I hung up and immediately dialed another number. "I'll be just a minute," I said to Max.

His lopsided grin was adorable. "Not a problem."

"Addison."

"Mitch, did Rich talk to you about a client of ours?"

"Yeah, a stalker case in my beat."

"The guy called again and was specific about what she was carrying. I was wondering if you could-"

Mitch interrupted me with a smile in his voice, "Keep a special eye out?"

"Yeah."

"Will do. Hey, haven't talked to you in a couple of days. How are you doing?"

"Tell Mom I'm fine, ya spy." I smiled at Max who looked puzzled but smiled back.

Mitch chuckled. "So you know. Okay the jig is up, but just so I know, how are you?"

"Fine."

"Tell Mitch hi for me," Max said.

"Who was that?" Mitch asked.

"Max Bauer. He's in town for a day or so."

"I see. Uh-huh. Tell him hi, and don't do anything I wouldn't do." There was a leering tone to his voice.

"Shut up." I hung up as Mitch began laughing.

I turned to Max as I returned the portable phone to its base. He was smiling that smile again.

He was adorable. His brown short hair was slightly messed, as though he had just gotten out of the shower. The tan polo shirt and jeans made him look sexy with just an air of sophistication.

"What?" he asked.

"What did you have in mind for tonight?" I got comfortable on the stool.

He shrugged. "I don't care, anything with you sounds like fun."

"Oh, come on. You flew all the way back here and you didn't have a plan?"

"The plan was to fly back here and see you." His smile increased. "I see you."

I chuckled. "I guess I should be flattered."

His smile lit the room. "So, what do you normally do on a Wednesday night here?"

"Well, let's see... usually I'm either working the bars on Front Street or I'm humping the streets near downtown." I grinned.

"A working woman. I like women who have their careers firmly in place."

"Yeah, but you couldn't afford me."

"Really?"

I shrugged. "I need to do laundry, but I think I can put that off. Want to get a drink downstairs?"

Max stood up. "'To the moon, Alice.'"

I chuckled all the way down the stairs. It was a slow night in the bar. Cam was working. Only three firefighters in tonight, and no cops.

"Hey, Mel?" one of the three called out to me as Max and I got settled at the bar.

"Yeah, Hank?" I smiled at Cam as he set two beers in front of us.

"I heard tell that you're going to start dating firefighters instead of those crafty cops. Is that true?" Hank moved to the bar with an empty pitcher. Cam chuckled under his breath as he grabbed the pitcher.

"Did Steve Wettle shoot off his mouth after I turned him down?"

Hank sat down next to me, looking past me to Max. "Bauer, right? Weren't you on the force a while back?"

Max extended his hand. "Yeah. Two months ago. Max Bauer."

Hank shook his hand. "Hank Gruber. Firefighter." He winked at Max. "Mel here is off cops, Max. She wants a real man."

Bauer glanced at him giving him a critical eye, then looked with the same type of glance at the other two firefighters. "Oh really!" He looked around the bar in general. There was only one other man here seated at the bar. "Then I don't have to worry. Besides Cam, I'm the only real man here."

The other firefighters hooted and groaned.

I shook my head at both of them as I gulped down the first swallow of ice cold beer.

"Real men play with fire, not flashing lights," Hank intoned as Cam brought the full pitcher back to him.

"Yeah, but cops like to do it with handcuffs." His eyes twinkled.

I stood up, grabbing my beer. I smiled at both men who looked at me, clearly puzzled. I moved down the bar and sat next to the other, older guy. He looked like he'd been around awhile. His face was lined in just the right way. "Don't you know guys, real women like men that are in it for the long haul, huh, Joe." I put my arm around his waist and laid my head on his shoulder.

Joe chuckled. He was a trucker and an old friend of the family's. He continued to sip his beer. As the silence drew out for a few seconds, he finally looked at the two men staring at us. "Use truckers have drive!"

The others cracked up laughing. Hank returned to his table. I kissed Joe on the cheek and headed back to sit next to Bauer. Max was totally amused by the whole thing. He tipped his bottle to me as I sat. Together we drank.

Later, after Cam went home leaving me to close the bar, it was just Joe, Max and myself. Joe stood and headed to the bathroom.

I sat across the bar from Max who was nursing his last beer. "So, why really did you come back to Quincy?"

His eyes snapped to mine. "To see you."

I cocked my head and smirked.

Max glanced in the direction of the bathroom. "Really. To see you. After the other night..." He drifted off as Joe approached from the back.

"Tell Dickie, I'll stop by next run through town," Joe handed me a twenty. "Keep the change, Mel." He winked at me with a slight nod to Max and left.

Max chuckled, swallowing the last of his beer.

I slid off the stool and moved around the bar to the empty tables. I tipped the first chair upside down on the table and soon Max was helping me. His grin was plastered on his face. I smiled. "Drink a bit too much?"

He chuckled then shrugged.

"Okay, Cowboy. No driving for you."

He paused. "Does that mean..." He lifted his eyebrows with a teasing smile on his face.

"Not likely, but you can sleep on my couch."

"Good enough."

After the bar was locked, we headed upstairs. Grabbing an extra blanket and pillow, I tossed them to Max who was emptying out his pockets on the coffee table. I sat down on the end of the couch and waited until he sat too.

"Well? Why did you come back here?"

He sobered some. "Your call the other night. You sounded freaked out. I was worried."

I gave him a slight smile.

"But I see all is well."

I nodded.

"At least on the outside." He stared into my eyes.

I just stared back.

"You still got issues though, huh?"

I just stared back.

"You know you can talk to me about anything."

I gave a very slight nod.

"Good." He grinned. "Wanna play twenty questions?"

I laughed myself into my bedroom.

***

I nudged Bauer awake on my couch. "Rise and shine, Handsome."

He grunted.

He looked precious sleeping on the couch. His hair tousled on the pillow, his blanket half on him and half on the floor. He was sleeping on his back with one arm and leg hanging off the couch, the other arm draped over his head. I smiled and moved off into the kitchen area of the common area.

As he stood up, stretching and yawning, he mumbled something to me in the kitchen.

I chuckled. "What was that?"

"What time is it?"

"Seven-thirty."

"Why am I awake?"

"I have to go to work today. Some of us aren't on vacation, you know."

"Okay, but why did you wake me?" He rubbed his eyes as he plopped down on a stool. "You could've just given me a kiss on the way out."

"With that breath?"

Blowing into his hand, he smelled his own breath. "Yuck." With a half yawn, half grin he spoke, "Do you have any Tylenol? And why aren't you hung over?"

"Took a Tylenol before my shower."

"You showered already? Where was I?"

"Sleeping on the couch where you belonged." I offered him a bagel. "Breakfast?"

He shook his head. "I'll grab something at Wettle's if you're in a hurry. Want to do lunch?"

"Sure. I'll call you and let you know when."

Max nodded as he smoothed his hair.

"Gorgeous," I said, watching him.

"I know it, Tiger." He smiled, looking around and patting his pockets.

I pointed at the coffee table in the living room. He grabbed his keys, wallet and cell phone, then followed me out the door. We stopped by his rental car. "Thanks for last night. That was fun. And comforting."

His smile was bright enough to compete with the rising sun. "My pleasure. Any time." He rubbed my arm with a wink.

Shaking my head at him, I jumped into my Jeep. Before heading to the office, I wanted to find the tree trimmer, Hilton Craser.

The two trucks were parked near the corner of 22nd and State Streets. The guys were looking up into the big Dogwood tree, pointing and obviously discussing how to bring the half dead tree down without hitting the brick house or destroying the kidney-shaped flower bed still in bloom. I had no clue which of the four men was Mr. Craser. I guessed it was the oldest in the group.

"Excuse me," I said walking up. The group turned as one, each eyeing me.

"Hi. Your office said that I could find you here. I'm looking for Hilton Craser." My eyes were on the oldest but it was one of the younger guys that answered me. I swallowed my surprise and smiled. "Can I ask you some questions in private? By the way, I'm Melissa Addison with Security Investigations." I held out my hand.

The others were quiet as Hilton tentatively shook my hand. "What about?"

"Please. It won't take long. I promise. Less than five minutes."

He glanced at his fellow workers and motioned with his hand to walk back toward my Jeep. He shrugged over his shoulder to the guys who went back to discussing the tree. "Yes?"

I glanced at the others, but they were mostly ignoring us. "Your name came up in an investigation of ours-"

"I swear I only cheated that once," Hilton began with a look of disbelief. "I can't believe she would hire a PI to look into this. We're divorced now. She got all my money, what else does she want from me?" Finally he stopped talking when I raised eyebrows. "You aren't here about that, are you?"

I shook my head.

"My ex-wife didn't hire you, did she?"

I shook my head.

"Now I'm embarrassed."

I chuckled, patting his arm. "Don't be. You'd be surprised how many times this has happened to me." It was a first for me too but I hoped it would be less embarrassing for him. "The reason I'm here is because I found your name in a book of a client's and we're trying to determine what the connections was."

Hilton's face looked puzzled. "Okay."

"Ruth Meddleson had your name in her little black notebook. How do you know her?"

"Ruth Meddleson? Isn't she the old lady that was killed a while back?"

I nodded and asked again, "How do you know her?"

He rubbed his chin. "I don't. I mean I have no idea- My number, huh?" He shook his head. Unfortunately, he looked totally puzzled by the idea. "Ruth Meddleson?"

"Older lady, mid sixties. Brown hair, dyed. About five ten. Didn't really look her age." Suddenly a light went on in his head. I could see it in his eyes. "Do you know her?"

"Not really. I think that might be the lady that I talked to about doing my step-dad's birthday party." He paused. "Older lady, but still a looker. Thin and in great shape."

I nodded. I had no idea. The only description I had of her was from the autopsy and the picture of her from Viking. I hadn't even seen any pictures of her in her house.

"It must be her. I called the company, and she called me back. I decided that maybe a good looking woman singing at his party would be too much for my step-dad after his recent heart surgery."

I blinked several times. *Singer? Ruth? Working as a singer at a party?* After getting a hold of myself, I asked, "What company?"

"Uh, I lived in St. Louis at the time. I just moved here three weeks ago." Hilton scratched his head. "Entertainment something. I saw an article on them in the newspaper there." He shrugged. "Sorry I can't help you out more."

"No." I looked past his shoulder to the street. After thinking for a moment, I focused back on him. "Actually, you've helped a lot. I appreciate you talking with me." I shook his hand. "Thanks."

My mind was a whirlwind as I drove to the office. It was becoming clear that Ruth Meddleson was not the spinster widow that her neighbors thought she was.

CHAPTER 12

I slid into my desk and did a quick search of the data bases for Entertainment Extravaganza. It was listed as a booking company for musical groups in the greater St. Louis area. *Okay, so the singer angle made sense.*

"Mel, phone call," Pam announced.

"Thanks." I picked up the phone. "Mel."

"Are we still on for Saturday night?" Bart Hessor's voice sounded smug.

"Well…" I hesitated. "Yeah. I guess."

"You guess?"

"I don't want you to get the wrong impression."

"I'm helping you, nothing more." Bart's voice was once again that slick, 'no strings attached, only helping you' voice.

I almost sighed in his ear, but my attention was centered on my doorway and the body filling its frame. Rich. And he was steaming mad. Again. "Look, can I call you back? Maybe tomorrow? I've got to go."

"Sure."

I hung up. His arctic blue eyes gleamed inflamed quartz. His body language like rigor mortis. His attitude, taunt wire tight. I could hear the twanging of fibers breaking in his head. I swallowed.

"Reverend Gordon Grace called." His tea pot was singing.

"So, fire me."

Rich turned red. Fists clenched. Eyes slits.

"Am I fired?"

"Get out of my face." Each word enunciated. An accusatory finger pointing to the front door.

I slowly stood, my eyes fastened to his. The tension ratcheted up. With deliberate movement, I collected my purse. We squared off at the doorway.

Rich not yielding. I crept to within inches of him. Eye to eye. Sister to brother. Icy blue meeting icy blue.

"Winnie is still missing."

His face, granite.

"Simon is innocent."

"Get out of here." Whisper soft and harsh.

I walked out without looking back. If Rich told the family, they would side with him. Dad and he always thought alike. Mitch was already mad at us. The only reason he agreed to do the drive-by at Roma's was because it was his job. Mom would go with Dad. Cam always tried to stay neutral. *This was not good.*

I drove away considering my options. *Rich was right. I have no reason to continue this investigation. None.* Yet, I knew that Simon was innocent. I knew it.

With a deep breath to release tension, I called Max. I needed a sympathetic ear.

"Yeah?"

"Hey, I got the morning off." I rubbed my neck. This lying was becoming a habit. I needed to stop, because it was getting way too easy. "Wanna do something?"

"Sure." Max was happy, I could tell by his voice. "I need to shower yet. Give me about half an hour. Do you know where Steve lives?"

"Yeah. I'll see you in about forty-five minutes."

"What are we doing?"

"Ever been to Hannibal, Max?"

"No. I never made it down there. Anything fun to see about Mark Twain?"

"Prepare to be Tom Sawyer'ed."

He chuckled as he hung up.

I dug into my file in the car and came up with the list of animal hospitals and veterinarians in Hannibal. Out of my fanny pack, I pulled the picture of Winnie. While I was there, I might as well check in with them, just in case. With time on my hands, I could re-canvas the Quincy vets starting tomorrow. It was the only lead I had.

***

"So, what can be so exciting about Mark Twain? He wrote a few books," Max said as he jumped in the Jeep.

"Didn't you have to read Tom Sawyer or The Adventures of Huckleberry Finn?"

"Well, yeah. In high school."

"The cave where Tom and Becky got lost?" I asked.

"It's real?"

"Sure as shooting."

"What?"

I laughed. "I need to make one stop first to confirm a card game on Friday. I can't reach Mr. Boden." I frowned. For two days I had tried to confirm with him, but he either wasn't returning my calls or he was gone.

The house was empty. Even Scruffy wasn't home. I walked around back and looked into the garage. His car was gone. With a puzzled look, I headed back to the Jeep.

"Problem?" Max asked with his arms crossed.

"He's not home."

"So?"

"Odd." I drove the four blocks to Mrs. Beaverton's house. She answered the door on the third knock.

"Mrs. Beaverton, I've been trying to reach Mr. Boden. Do you know where he is?"

"He got a call from his daughter in Chicago. I think he went there for a couple of days." Her face was more lined then the last time and she looked rather pale. Maybe she wasn't wearing any make-up.

"Are you okay, Mrs. Beaverton?"

A sniffle. "Yes."

I quickly glanced to Max in the Jeep, who was watching. Turning back to her, I saw that she was on the verge of tears. "Mrs. Beaverton?"

"I think Earl is mad at me." That opened the flood gates and the tears flowed. She sucked in her breath trying to stop the emotion.

I put my arm around her and headed her back into the house. Over my shoulder, I saw Max starting to get out. I shook my head, motioning that I'd only be a minute.

"He's mad at me." Slipped out between halting breaths.

"Why do you think that?" I asked as we sat down on her couch.

"He's been cold these past couple of days, except at the card game the other night." She took the Kleenex that I held out from her box on the couch. She had obviously been crying for awhile. "Earl and I usually get together and watch a movie on Monday nights. He didn't want to, I could tell."

I patted her arm and made comforting sounds.

"Then he... he..." She stopped suddenly.

"What?"

"I can't talk about it."

"I'm a good listener, Mrs. Beaverton."

"I can't because I don't want anyone to- It's not that I... You being so young..." She again tried to stifle her sobs.

"I won't tell anyone. It'll stay right here between us."

Stella looked me in the eyes as she wiped hers. She seemed to be sizing me up as she took several deep breaths. "You wouldn't understand. You're so young. It's different after you've been married, but you wouldn't know what I'm talking about."

I shook my head. "Mrs. Beaverton, I was married. My husband died in a car accident eight months ago."

"I'm so sorry." This seemed to be an automatic response, like saying 'God bless you'.

"If I can help in any way…"

Her eyes were still measuring me. She wiped them once more as she got a hold of herself. "Earl and I have been having an affair for a few years. Actually a good number. My Horace died ten years ago. Yvonne, Earl's wife, got sick about the same time. Cancer, you know." Her eyes took on a glazed look. "When Yvonne got too sick, Earl took care of her. But she was too sick to do *anything*." The slate gray eyes caught mine.

I nodded in understanding.

"Earl, well, Earl is a *man,* you know. And he, we… At first, I felt so bad. I mean his wife was still alive, but she was just a shell. Then he had to move her into a nursing home, because it got to be too much for him. We… when Yvonne died, Earl was distraught. He would hardly talk or anything for the longest time. I always knew he loved her, and that I was just a-" Stella blushed. "Anyway, he put her death behind him. We continued. Well, a woman has *needs* too. I needed a man to help and Earl is so good to me."

"I'm sure he's not mad at you. He's probably just worried about his daughter or something."

"Probably," Stella said softly. "But I don't know."

"Why?"

"Woman's intuition. Last Monday, well, he started, but well, he occasionally has had problems before… in that department…" Almost embarrassed she lifted her hand then let it fall limp.

I started to cringed but stopped myself, not wanting to hurt her feelings. This was way too much information. I didn't want or need these images running around in my head.

"He wouldn't even kiss me. He said he had too many other things on his mind." Stella turned to me with another sniffle. "The last time he was this way was when his wife died. I understood then, but… he's too manly to not want to…." She shook her head. "I must have said or done something." A sniffle broke free.

"Mr. Boden would never hurt you in that way, Mrs. Beaverton. I'm sure when he gets back this will all be cleared up."

"Yeah. You're probably right, Mel." She smiled, wiping her almost dry eyes. "Thanks."

I stood. "Just call me and let me know if we are still on for Friday. Okay?"

Stella rose slowly. As she walked me to the door, she patted my back. "You're a good friend, Mel. I appreciate you stopping by and checking on me. Thanks for listening."

We said our goodbyes and I hurried to the Jeep. She waved one more time then went back into the house. I drove off.

"What was that about?"

I shuttered. "Oh man, she told me about her and Earl. Doing it. The images-" I shook myself all over. "Yucky."

Max started laughing. "Lots of old people do *it*. Did you think they just stopped after the kids were grown and out of the house?"

"No. I know they do. But..." I shuddered again. "It's like walking in on your grandparents doing it. The lose skin, the sagging bodies, the-" I did another whole body quake.

"That's the second time you've said that. Did you walk in on your grandparents doing it?"

I flashed him a look. "Yeah. It was disgusting. Yuck. Trust me. Almost put me off of *it*, too."

Max laughed so hard I thought he was going to wet himself. Finally, he wiped his eyes. "You do make my day, Mel." He reached over and squeezed my shoulder.

***

Max grinned as I exited the last veterinarian office in Hannibal. He was sitting with his arms crossed, a brochure of several Mark Twain attractions sitting in his lap.

I climbed in the Jeep.

"Anything?"

"Nope. No Winnie."

"Boy, I never knew Mark Twain loved his animals like he did." He winked. "I'm glad you showed me all of the veterinarian offices here in Hannibal. I would never have thought..."

I smirked.

"What else is going on?"

"What?"

"You've had a semi-sour look on your face all morning." He settled deeper into the seat, then changed the subject. "I'm hungry. Let's stop somewhere."

I headed to a local restaurant.

After we ordered, he reached across the table and patted my hand. "Spill."

I shook my head.

He scrunched his face. "Don't leave me remembering you all sour and upset. I want to remember a happy and smiling Mel."

I gave him a fake smile.

He shook his head then stuck out his tongue at me.

I chuckled.

"Much better. Now what's the problem?"

"Rich fired me."

"What?"

I nodded, fiddling with the napkin. "He wants me to stop looking for Winnie."

Max didn't speak for several long seconds. "Let me guess, he actually wants you to stop looking into Simon's case?"

I gawked. *How did he know that?*

Max gave me a wry grin. "When I tracked you down yesterday, Rich mentioned it."

I cursed under my breath.

Max laughed. "I won't tell Rich that you're still looking for 'the doggie', but-"

"Not you too!"

He nodded. "Your brother has to know that once you get a hold of something, you're like a pit bull." He mimed as though he bit into something then shook his head. "And I've learned in the short time I've known you, that trying to get you to stop is, well, useless. So-"

I rolled my eyes. "Here it comes…"

He lifted my hand and kissed it gently, more of a caress with his lips. "Be careful."

Be careful. Good advice. But what about the shivers running up and down my spine? Careful of what, the case or him?

Later in the afternoon we stood next to Max's rental. He needed to leave if he was going to make his flight in St. Louis. He had been great company all day.

"Remember what I said." He left his 'be careful' remark hanging in the air. "And next time, we'll have to do more of Mark Twain, you know, more of the actual touristy stuff," Max said tossing his overnight bag into the front seat.

I smirked.

"Good luck finding the 'little Shih Tzu'," Max said, after he closed the passenger door.

"Yeah."

His blue eyes met mine. They seemed to be delving deep into my soul. The tension grew. But this tension felt warm, comforting and oh so irresistible. *Move on. Keep it friendly. Don't give in.* I cleared my throat. "I had fun. Thanks for coming to see me."

Max just nodded. A smile played at his lips.

"What?" I asked as he moved closer to me until we were less than an inch apart.

"If I kissed you-"

"I'd haul off and hit you." I finished for him as my heart raced faster and my body screamed 'Yes!'

"That's what I thought." He sighed softly. "Will you still consider coming out and seeing me?"

"Maybe."

Max reached out and traced my chin with his finger. Feather soft. A butterfly touch. "I gotta go."

I took a step back to let him pass, fighting the feelings, the urges, the passion. His eyes were intent, still staring at me, my heart doing the two-step. *I can't let him go like this. I want...* I stopped him, lightly touching his arm. With a smirky grin I leaned closer, "Can you help me with one thing?"

His expression got puzzled.

"I need to erase an image."

"Of?"

I did a whole body shudder.

He cracked up laughing.

I hastily gave him a kiss on the lips. Just a peck.

He responded by cradling my head. He leaned into me. His lips caressing mine. His tongue just barely exploring my mouth. Slowly he pulled away from me, our lips the last thing to separate except for his gentle hold on the sides of my face around my ears. Then with a deliberate slowness, he caressed my cheeks. The last touch was of his index finger giving me the 'shshhh' sign on my tingling lips. "But I won't hit you." His eyes twinkled.

I smiled.

He leaned in close. "You're a great kisser," he whispered, his soft breath in my ear. He reached out and once more traced my chin with a fingertip. "Until next time." He slid into the car.

I watched as he drove away, my insides on fire. His breath had caused heat to rise in places I thought were dead. My heart swelled.

I felt tranquil. I felt calm. I felt unburdened.

***

The next day Gordon Grace wasn't answering my phone calls. *Why had he called me back?* The drive past his house/office was useless; he wasn't there.

Roma wasn't home either. I left a message on her voice mail to call me and let me know how things were going.

I tried Entertainment Extravaganza again, but got the answering machine. I didn't leave a message. I closed my cell phone. *What to do next?*

I needed more information about Ruth. I jumped up and headed to my Jeep. I knocked on Beaverton's door once more.

She met me with a smile. "Earl called from Chicago," Stella said as she ushered me into the house. "His daughter was in the hospital. He won't be back until probably Sunday. He said he wants to spend some time with her. So I guess Friday night is off."

There was another lady sitting in the living room. I smiled at her. She sort of nodded back.

"Oh Mel, this is Eugenia Hamilton."

As I sat I held out my hand to her. "Hi, Mrs. Hamilton."

"You were the one looking into getting Simon out of jail." The tone was condescending.

"I was. Now, I'm just looking for Winnie." *Liar, lair pants on fire.* I turned to Beaverton. "I'm glad things worked out."

Stella sat with a knowing grin at Hamilton. "Earl is such a dear, uh Eugenia?"

"Stella!"

Stella chuckled. She patted Hamilton on the arm. "Mel knows about me and Earl."

Eugenia blushed a deep shade of red.

I hesitated. "Do you also have a…"

Stella nodded at me. She sort of blushed too. "Earl is *the man* in the neighborhood. We all kind of share him."

I wanted to shudder again. I didn't want to hear this. I wanted to put my hands in my ears and sing 'la, la, la, la', to myself. "I see."

Hamilton gave a slight nod, still embarrassed. "Earl is very sweet." She gave me another condescending look. "You just wait, young lady. Women outnumber men four to one at our age. And those men our age generally have trouble getting, well, they just have trouble. If you get my meaning. Earl is *very* good. We agreed, Stella and me, that instead of fighting over our Earl, we would share him."

I took a breath instead of doing the full-body shudder. "Sounds like a wise thing to do. I'll remember that when I get to be your age."

That got the ladies giggling.

I smiled. "I want to ask you some questions about Ruth." I paused as Stella opened her mouth. "I'm hoping that if I can find out more about Ruth, I might be able to find Winnie."

"But Earl said he was at Ruth's niece's house."

"He isn't. Where did Ruth work?"

"She used to work for an insurance company. She did those physical check things. You know, she went around and checked on people before they got insurance. Blood pressure and stuff. Before that…" Stella paused to think. "I think she was a tutor. She was always gone in the evening and nights. When she retired, she was forever traveling. Not far though. She said she enjoyed the tri-state area."

"St. Louis?"

Stella sipped at the tall glass with an amber liquid. "Ruth loved St. Louis. She knew that city like we know Quincy. I always wondered why she never moved there. Did she ever tell you, Eugenia?"

"Once. When Simon was younger. She didn't want to raise him in the big city. She thought a small town environment was better for raising kids." Eugenia shook her head sadly, picking up an identical glass. "Didn't seem to do much good in Simon's case though. I guess once a bad seed, always bad."

"Did she ever have a lover after her husband died?"

"Not that I know of. She was a strong woman. Very independent." Stella fluffed the pillows next to her, then took another drink. "Only occasionally did Earl ever go over to help her out. Usually just outside things. I remember once he helped her get a raccoon out of her chimney." Stella chuckled. "Oh my, I remember it took them a week working on it. The stupid critter just wouldn't budge. Remember, Eugenia? They tried from the inside, too." Both ladies started giggling again.

Were these women drunk? I saw that both of their glasses were almost empty. I've seen many drunks, and these two were definitely buzzing. *Wait.* I narrowed my eyes. "Mrs. Beaverton, Ruth didn't have a fireplace."

"This was years ago, Mel. Before my Horace passed away, God rest his soul." Stella patted her heart. "Ruth had the fireplace taken out when Simon became fascinated with fire." She leaned closer. "I think she was afraid that Simon would burn the house down." She giggled.

I frowned.

"What was the company's name that she worked for and how long ago was it?"

"Oh, years. A good five or seven, easy." Stella thought. "I don't ever know if I ever knew the company name. Ruth was a friend, but she was very private with her home life. Earl would know more. He helped all of us ladies in the neighborhood. Ruth might have confided in him."

"Thanks for the information."

"How will it help find Winnie?"

"I'm not sure to be honest with you, Mrs. Beaverton. I'm just getting a feel for the whole family."

"Do you think Simon killed Winnie too?" Eugenia asked.

I hesitated. "Honestly, everything points to that. And everyone thinks so. I don't know. Something's not right. I haven't given up yet. I just hope Winnie is still alive and well. Thanks for your help, ladies."

Beaverton showed me to the door.

I headed down the street and stopped at the Allen's. Maybe they might know more. Frank showed me into the kitchen where Mary, who was using a walker, was cooking supper.

"I won't take much of your time."

"That's okay. I'm late making lunch anyway," Mrs. Allen said as she turned down the boiling water. She slid some sort of vegetables into the water as I walked in. "Frank said that you were looking for Winnie."

"I'm stuck and I'm trying a new tack. Maybe Simon gave the dog to someone from her past. His dog bowls were gone too. I was wondering if you knew who she used to work for?"

The two older people looked at each other.

"Mrs. Beaverton thought it was some sort of insurance agency health check thing. At least, recently that is. Before that she was a tutor."

Both were nodding in agreement. "The insurance thing always was a puzzler," Frank said with a glance at Mary. "We've always doubted that story."

"Story?"

"The hours were too odd. She was always gone in the evenings and weekends." Frank took a drink of his coffee.

"Then what did she do?"

Another look passed between them. Mary cleared her throat. "I guess it wouldn't hurt to tell now."

I waited.

"We never did confirm this, mind you," Mary qualified.

"I understand."

"We've always believed that she had a gentleman that she visited. You know, someone that she would see at odd times. She never hurt for money, although she didn't flaunt it. I have always thought that she was having an affair with a married man."

"Did you have any proof of it?"

The same look passed again between the them. Frank nodded at Mary. "Tell her. It can't cause any harm now."

"Okay. One time I was sitting on the back porch, right after my stroke, and I heard her arguing with a man."

"In her house?"

Mary nodded. "This was a year ago maybe. It wasn't Simon. As a matter of fact, it was right before he showed up again."

"What were they arguing about?"

"That's the funny thing," Mary said. Her eyes took on a thoughtful look. "They were arguing about her moving."

I waited, letting her think back. I could tell she was struggling to remember.

"Let's see. The man kept saying something about it would be easier on everyone if she moved closer to St. Louis, as that was where his action was."

"Where his action was?"

"He said something like, 'I live there… You should live there, it would be easier on the action or with my action.' Or something like that. I think. It's been awhile now."

"Hmm."

"It got quite loud. He called her some pretty nasty names, too. The one in particular I remember was… I haven't forgotten that one." Mary hesitated then turned a tad red. "Whore."

"Anything else?"

"No. The fight turned to money, I think. I didn't want to pry so I went back inside." Mary smoothed her hair.

"Was he younger or older than her?"

"I didn't see them."

"What did he sound like, age-wise?"

"I don't really remember. He didn't sound like Simon's age, I can tell you that. So, I guess older. I think."

I needed to justify this in response to the dog. "Was this before or after Winnie was around?"

"Oh, before," Mary said. "Maybe." She looked down at her walker.

"It was after, Mary," Frank said. "Simon brought Winnie home for Christmas the year it snowed really heavily, remember? We were surprised by his strange car parked in the alley. It blocked our garage."

"No. I'm sure it was before. I would remember if I heard Winnie barking. You remember how he barked up a storm the night I had my stroke. Barking and barking at the sirens. I remember."

"And he did. Ruth had Winnie longer than a year, Mary. He couldn't get to the grassy area, two winters ago because he was so small. I had to shovel a path from her door to the backyard after that heavy snow fall knocked the branch out of the tree. Remember?"

"That was last year, Frank. With all the ice. I slipped and feel on the patio. Shortly before my stroke."

I looked from one to the other. They were shaking their heads at each other. Mary was stabbing her finger at the table. Frank was pointing out the back door. "Uh... it really doesn't matter, Mrs. Allen..."

"It does. I'm right. It was before."

"After, Mary." Frank turned to me. "She has a hard time remembering things after the stroke."

"Don't blame my stroke for your crummy memory. You have always forgotten things." Mary raised her voice even louder.

I stood up. "Well, thank you for the information, anyway."

They both nodded at me and continued the argument. I made a quick exit. I could hear them still arguing through the open window as I sat in my Jeep. With an exhale, I smiled. At least they had each other to fight with.

Back home, I reviewed the police file again. Nothing struck my fancy. I reread the autopsy report. Nothing. With a sigh, I even reread our file in case I had missed something.

A note in John's paperwork caught my eye. I had never heard the guys discussing this. Jeffery Ledbecker, a.k.a. Punky, had a list of priors as long as Simon's. And like Simon, they were mostly minor charges. Except one. He had been charged with vehicular manslaughter. It had been dropped due to 'strange circumstances'.

Everything in St. Louis tied in with Punky and, on the outskirts, Rascals. My search had revealed that Rascals was merely a dance club, a very popular dance club with the younger generation. The owners were a corporation and I had had trouble getting a list of the board members.

I looked out my window into the darkness. Now that I no longer had access to the data bases at the office, it could get really hard to get information. Maybe I should invest in a laptop at home. I needed to get connected to the internet anyway.

I headed to bed with thoughts of which laptop I should buy, but they all fled when I laid my head next to Petey on the pillow. The ache in my heart opened again. Once more I cuddled him to me for comfort.

I'd drifted off when my phone scared me. "Hello?"

"Mel, he's here. He's here."

"Roma, calm down." I could hear her breathing faster and faster. "Calm down and tell me what happened."

"Okay." Roma took a deep breath. "I came home from work. Everything was normal. And there was another message on the machine from him. He said that he liked the dress I wore tonight at the book store."

I felt so bad for her. This had to be terrifying.

"I made myself a late supper and read my mail. There was a note from him. I opened it. He told me my routine for the last week. You know, I wasn't even shocked. Anyway, it was mailed from here in town. The post mark says so. I set it aside to show Detective Hawkings. He's due here tomorrow morning to talk to me about getting the restraining order."

I moved into the kitchen for a drink of water. My head was stuffy and my throat was tingling. I hoped I wasn't coming down with a cold.

"Just two minutes ago, there was a knock at my door. I looked out the peep. Devon smiled at me. Then he laid a package at my door." Roma inhaled a deep breath. "What do I do, Mel?"

"Don't retrieve the package. Don't open the door. Why didn't you call 911?"

"I don't know why. I'm scared." Roma took a shaky breath. "He's never done that before."

I frowned. I was in over my head. "Make sure your door is locked tight. Sit by the phone. Let me call Rich. Then one of us will call you back. Okay?"

"Hurry. I'm really scared, Mel."

"Sit tight." I hung up and glanced at the clock. It was only eleven. Rich was probably still up. My sister-in-law answered the phone.

"Hi, Gloria." I put a smile in my voice. "Sorry for calling so late. Can I speak to Rich?" I heard Gloria tell Rich who it was. I swallowed.

"Mel." The tone hadn't changed.

"Hi,Rich."

"Apologizing?"

"Huh, no. Roma called. Devon appeared on her doorstep and left her something about two minutes ago. She's really stressed out. I told her one of us would call her back with what to do. What do I tell her?"

There was a pause.

"I have no idea what to do, Rich. Should she call the police or just wait? He left a package outside her door."

"Sorry that she bothered you. I'll have her call John or myself from now on." The phone died on me.

He had never, ever been this mad before. It was scary. *But what could I do?* I felt compelled to help Simon. I knew he was innocent. I couldn't live with myself if he went to prison when I knew he didn't kill his mom. Now I felt like I had betrayed Roma. I wanted to help her too but I couldn't do that until I made peace with Rich. And I couldn't do that until I found out about Ruth's murder.

Cursing softly I dug into my purse and stared at a business card. It was the fastest way to get information, the kind of information that wasn't in any databases. I knew what I had to do. With a heavy heart, I dialed the number. I knew Bart would still be up.

"Bart, how about tomorrow night instead?"

CHAPTER 13

Pam called first thing in the morning. It sounded like she was whispering. "Mel, you got a call a minute ago."

"Yeah?"

"Vincent Viking called. Wants you to call him back." She hesitated. "Look, I don't want to anger Rich. I need this job."

"Thanks for the call Pam. From now on tell Rich. He can't fire me more than he already has."

"But-"

"Seriously, don't endanger your job because of me."

"All you have to do is-"

"I know, Pam. Don't get involved. Thanks again."

She sighed. "Okay."

I dialed Viking's office. "This is Melissa Addison. Vincent wanted to talk to me."

It wasn't long before the lawyer was on the phone. Even he sounded reluctant to talk to me. I knew he didn't know about my troubles with Rich, but he still didn't sound happy. "I'm calling on behalf of Simon. He wants you to visit him at the jail. Today, if possible. I listed you on the approved contact list. He said it was important."

I frowned. "Did he say why?"

"I can guess."

"Then guess, Mr. Viking."

"I've struck a deal with the district attorney's office. All it requires is Simon's approval. It's a good deal for him, better than I thought I could get."

"But?"

"I think he wants to talk to you about it. He seems to trust you a great deal."

"Okay." I drug out each syllable.

"Reassure him that this is a good deal. It truly is."

"I'll try."

I had so much to do today. If I was going to squeeze Simon's visit in, I would need to get going. Reluctantly, I headed to the shower.

***

The wait at the jail was longer then I expected, so I would need to cut my list of vets in the city in half. I knew that the longer it took me to quiz the staff at the various animal hospitals, the worse people's memories would get. This was my only lead, or at least my best one.

Finally, Simon was shown into the room. He sat down and with his beady eyes, stared at me. "What have you found?"

"Not much."

He cursed loudly.

"Viking said he cut a deal for you. He says it's a good one."

Simon nodded as he looked off into the corner. Finally, he brought his gaze back to me. "I know it is, but it requires that I confess to Mom's murder. No one believes me but you. I didn't kill my mom."

I didn't know what to say.

"Viking says it'll be bargained down to voluntary manslaughter. Twenty-five years. I'll probably serve only ten to fifteen if I behave." Simon rubbed his hands together, then cracked his knuckles. "It's not the time. I've gotten away with enough stuff to cover four life times. But I didn't kill my mom. And the deal will only happen if I confess."

I leaned on the table. "One of the neighbors heard your mom arguing with a guy several months ago, maybe longer. He wanted her to move to St. Louis. He called her a bunch of names. Who was he? Do you know?"

Simon's eyes betrayed the fact he knew exactly who the guy was. Simon shook his head. "I dunno."

"Simon, I can't find the real killer if you aren't up front with me. Who was this guy? Was he angry enough to kill her after so long?"

Without hesitation, he shook his head. "Nah. Mom and him patched things up."

"What's his name?"

"Buddy. Don't know his last name." He was still lying.

"From St. Louis?"

Simon nodded.

"Were they lovers?"

"Could have been."

I frowned. "You're seriously hobbling me. I need all the information, if you want me to help you."

"It wasn't Buddy."

"How do you know?"

"Buddy's dead."

"Dead? When?"

"The same night Mom died." Simon smirked. "I just know. Look, keep trying. I have to let Viking know about the deal Monday morning by noon." Simon's eyes burned into mine. "Can you come back here Monday morning before noon?"

"I'll do my best."

He held out his hand and we shook. "I know. That's why I hired you." With a wink, he was at the door calling for the guard.

***

I arranged to meet Bart at his bar. I didn't want him anywhere near Dad's place. Heaven forbid any of my family saw me out with a Hessor. Besides the Rich thing not sitting well, this would get me kicked out of the family so fast, it would make my buried, grandfather's skull launched right out of his grave. I parked my Jeep at the twenty-four hour grocery store two blocks away and walked.

"Mel, you look great," Bart said as soon as he saw me. His eyes tracing up and down.

I glanced down. I was dressed in a pair of dress black pants and a slinky black top. It was shiny and loose fitting with spaghetti straps. The jacket over top of it made for a more conservative look. I didn't want to give him too much to see.

"Ready to go? I thought we'd take my car. You know, save on gas."

"I guess. Will Punky be there?"

Bart nodded as he led the way, guiding me to his green jaguar. As he opened the door, he intoned, "One of my guys down there said he'd make sure Punky showed up."

I almost rolled my eyes. Bart was strong-arming a source of information. I bet I wouldn't get any information from him.

The two and a half hour drive to St. Louis was fun, I hate to admit. Bart and I always did have fun together. We traded stories of the 'old days' as teens. He told me of some other funny things that had happened to him. Details of his travels came out as we talked. He regularly visited Mexico and even further south. By the time we reached Rascals, I was fairly comfortable with him again. It was like it was back in high school, only I was much more in control now. And aware.

Bart led me up to the door of Rascals, skipping the line. The bouncer addressed him by name and let us in without any hesitation. I was impressed to say the least. Bart took my hand and led me through the crowded floor. He stopped at the bar, where the bartender immediately waited on us. Bart got a micro-brew for me and a mixed drink for himself. I couldn't hear what it was because of the loud music.

The music was not the kind I listen to, but it had a good beat. My eyes scanned the crowd, checking out the tables along the perimeter and the packed dance floor.

Two whole walls were mirrors. There were a lot of gyrating bodies out there, with scantily clad woman doing the bump and grind with some decent looking guys. I was impressed. It seemed to attract a fairly upscale crowd. I couldn't imagine Simon hanging out here.

"What?" I called back to Bart. A new song just started.

"I said, let's see if my contact is here yet." He took my hand again. He made a path through the crowd and headed to the back corner of the club where the mirrored walls met.

We went straight for a set of double doors in the rear. Standing in front of them like a guard, was a big, burly black man. Muscularly huge. I bet he could bench press a car. His eyes swung back and forth in front of him, watching, cataloging. Intelligent eyes. Wary eyes.

I noticed that when they focused on Bart, they became intensely focused on him, only him. He stiffened, almost at a military attention.

"Mr. Hessor," he greeted us as we got near. Since we were further away from the speakers we didn't have to yell at each other.

"Hi, Randy. This is Mel."

Randy inclined his head.

"Is Halbert here yet?"

"No, sir. I haven't seen him."

Hessor nodded with a glance back to the dance floor. "When he shows up, have him come right in. Thanks, Randy," Bart said as Randy stepped out of our way and opened the door.

I glanced with a smile at Randy as Bart and I went through the double doors. When Randy closed them behind us, the noise was cut in half.

Bart smiled at me and led me up a small set of stairs to one of the many booths in front of a huge window. This was the other side of the mirrored wall. The booths had tall sides extending close to the ceiling, so that each booth was almost a small room. "This is the VIP area. I reserved one of the last booths. We can watch all the action while we wait for Halbert and Punky."

Before sitting I looked around again. Several of the booths were already occupied. And in one we had passed, the couple was engaged in more than casual conversation. It was steamy in that booth. I glanced at Bart.

He gave me a wry grin. His blond hair stood in the dim room; the blue of his eyes flashing amusement. "Not to worry, Mel. I don't have those sort of intentions tonight, unless you want to." He raised an eyebrow.

I made a noise in my throat and he laughed. We settled into the booth. I leaned on the table, looking closer at the undulating bodies in front and slightly below us.

"Sometimes it's fun to watch all the body language out there," Bart said tipping his drink toward the outer area.

"Do you come here a lot?"

Bart chuckled. "I have too. I own the place."

"Excuse me?"

Bart laughed. "Three of us own it. These last three booths are ours." His finger flipped to the other two booths near the wall, both unoccupied. "I do a lot of business here."

"I bet."

"Now, now. Let's not start out on a bad footing. I won't mention my other business again."

"Good," I said as I sipped my beer.

His family and mine had been at odds for years. While Bart and I were teens, and secretly dating, my Dad arrested his Aunt dealing drugs. Since then Bart has taken over for his Aunt, or whoever was in charge after she 'left'. Rich had 'taken over' for my Dad and had many times tried to arrest Bart for dealing drugs. Only once had he come close.

Needless to say, my family would not approve of me being on this date, even just to get information. Only John knew of my past with Bart, and he was keeping it a secret.

"So," Bart began. "Why do you want to talk to Punky?"

I let my gaze rest on Bart for the longest time before answering him. The idea that Bart was playing me was never far from my mind. I didn't trust him, so I certainly wasn't going to give him a straight answer.

I swore after this case was over, I would never lie again. "Simon wants me to ask him something."

Bart's eyes were thoughtful.

I could tell he didn't fully believe me. Time to change the subject. "Have you ever heard of Entertainment Extravaganza?"

Bart nodded as he sipped from his glass.

"What exactly do they do?"

"Book music groups here at the Center or in the area."

"So their website says," I replied softly.

"You want to know what they *really* do?"

"Yeah."

Bart fingered his glass studying me. "I'll tell you what..." I knew this couldn't be good. "Come back with me tomorrow night, I have a party going on in the back room here..." He thumbed over his shoulder to another set of doors as he continued to speak, "Wendell, one of the owners of Entertainment Extravaganza, will be here. You can ask him all of your questions then. Deal?"

"Why do you want me here tomorrow?"

"For the party."

"Na huh. What's the real reason?"

Bart's smiled again. "You caught me. I need a gorgeous woman on my arm tomorrow night. All you have to do is wear something nice..." His eyes traced my body again. "Something like this. Drink. Have a good time, but don't question my guests too much. Okay?"

"Let me think about it."

The night turned out to be a bust. We waited until one but Halbert called and said that Punky hadn't met him as promised. Bart was not happy. He told Halbert to track Punky down and make sure he was here tomorrow night by ten. No excuses. The tone in his voice was cold, deadly cold. Bart was not a person I'd want mad at me.

***

I was standing at the small bar in the back room the next night getting a beer when Bart slid next to me. Tonight, I was dressed in the same outfit from the night before minus the light jacket. I'd slipped my ID and money into a small ankle holder, just in case.

"Punky and Halbert are in my booth. If you don't want to talk with Halbert around, ask him to step away. When you're done, make sure that Halbert escorts Punky out the door," Bart whispered into my ear.

I backed away with a 'stop that' kind of look.

Bart smiled. With a wink, he started to leave. "When you're done, come back in here. Wendell said he'd be here around eleven. I'll be over by the far tables. Come find me." He moved off, greeting several people as he made his way, schmoozing through the room.

I frowned but started toward the main door. I didn't like being used, but it was providing me access to the people I needed to see, and in an environment that they couldn't trace me. So, I guess since I was using Bart too, it was only fair.

Punky was wringing his hands. When he saw me, he looked behind me. After making sure that I wasn't being followed, he relaxed a bit. But only a tad.

"Thanks, Mr. Halbert. I'd like to talk with Punky alone please."

Halbert gave a slight bow and a warning look at Punky.

"Jeff, my name is Mel. Have a seat. I'm work for Simon Meddleson."

"Yeah? So?"

"Simon's about to go to prison for a long time for killing his mom. He says he was with you." I noticed Punky was already shaking his head. "Look, I know Simon's innocent. I just need proof. If you verify that he was with you here-"

"I was... He wasn't with me. No way, man."

I narrowed my eyes. He was extremely frightened about something. He rubbed his hands, his nose and then his hands again.

"I'm telling you-" Punky hesitated looking around. He lowered his voice. "Look, Simon's okay. He's good you know. He'll be okay in prison."

"That may be, but if he's innocent-"

"He didn't kill his mom, if that's what you mean."

"What do *you* mean?"

"What? I'm just saying..." Punky shoved his hands into his pockets for a split second then pulled them out to wring them again. He glanced around, looking especially at the door I had just come through. His eyes flicked back to me. "If I tell you what I know, you'll tell- you'll like tell Mr. Hessor I cooperated and everything, right? And no one else hears what I say, right?""

I nodded.

Punky glanced out the glass-fronted windows still nervous. He flicked his eyes to the door, to me, then back out to the dancers.

I cleared my throat which made him jump. I smiled. "Jeff, I wouldn't tell anyone what you tell me here tonight, I promise. Just tell the truth."

"Uh... Uh, well." His eyes once more made the circuit. With the way he was still wringing his hands, he should have been drawing blood by now. "Okay, but I'll deny I told you."

"Of course."

"Simon didn't kill his Mom 'cause like he killed someone else that night."

"Excuse me?"

Punky nodded so violently I thought I could hear his brain sloshing. "He did. He killed a man, here in St. Louis."

"So you were with him?"

"No. No. I was... I was... here at the club. Yeah, I was here."

I smiled, he was such a horrible liar. "Who and where?"

"Why?"

"So I can substantiate his claims."

"With 'nother murder?" Punky's voice sounded very puzzled. "How's that gonna help him?"

"I just need to find out if there was a murder the same night here. Give me some details."

"Uh... Uh, well. Okay, I guess. A man was shot by the water front. In the head. Then we, he, Simon pitched him into the river. The cops found his body yesterday. The car was found two days ago. In the airport parking lot. Simon parked it there, thinking it wouldn't be found right away. A green four door Honda."

"The guys name?"

"Cecil Weeks." Punky glanced around even as he lowered his voice. "Better known in the industry as Buddy."

No. No way. Simon couldn't have killed his mom because he was down in St. Louis killing Buddy, the guy who yelled at his mom. This was getting complicated, but it made sense. My mind flashed back to the jail cell and Simon's smirk.

"I'm not lying."

"I know," I said softly. Nervously, I ran a hand through my hair. *What did I do now?* "Okay, Jeff. Why did he kill Buddy?"

"I dunno."

"You're lying."

"Okay. Uh… uh, well… Okay, I only know it was personal between 'em. That's all I know."

I hesitated. *Had I gotten all of the information out of him?* I was sure that once he left I would never see him again, short of being summoned like this again. By Bart. With force. With strings attached. "Okay."

Punky gave me a nervous grin. "You'll tell Mr. Hessor?"

"I will."

Punky stood. "If you see Simon, tell 'em that everything's going as planned. As long as he keeps his bargain, I'll keep mine."

I motioned to Halbert. "When I see him, I'll pass it along. Thanks, Punky."

With a nod, he hurried away as though someone was chasing him. Halbert followed close at his heels.

I sat staring out the glass 'window' onto the dance floor. *What did I do with this information? If I told Viking, how were we to claim his innocence in killing his mom without indicting him in the murder of Buddy? And would Viking even want to know about this? If it was that important, why hadn't Simon told Viking himself? Any information between client and attorney is privileged and Viking wouldn't have been able to act on it anyway. Was there a reason Simon was keeping silent about this other murder?*

I scratched my head. Well, I could with a clean conscience make up with Rich now. That was a good thing. I might not be able to prove that Simon was innocent, but at least *I knew* he didn't murder his mom.

With a shake of my head, I went back to the party. There were two things that still bothered me. *Where was Winnie? And, who had killed Ruth?*

I wondered around then Bart waved me over to him. "Mel, this is Wendell Sterngis," Bart introduced us.

I held out my hand to the rather short, fat guy standing in front of me. His glasses were the latest in fashion, but they looked wrong on him. I would have put him in big, black, geek glasses. That would have made him much more comfortable looking.

Wendell smiled as we shook hands. "You've called me."

I smiled back and taking him by the arm, walked him away from Hessor and the bar. "I did. I'd like to ask you some questions." I glanced over my shoulder and saw that Bart had a strange look on his face. It looked like jealousy, maybe, or surprise. I wasn't sure and I really didn't care.

Wendell was nodding as he put his arm around my waist. "For a pretty lady like yourself, I'm always available. I knew that your voice sounded sexy, but you more than match the recording."

"Good try, Wendell." I stopped as we got closer to the wall and took his hand off my waist. There was no one near us here in the corner. "I found a letter from your business in my client's mail. I need to know if she worked for you or why she had a letter from you. Can you do that for me?"

He sipped his drink, then motioned to go on.

"Ruth Meddleson."

Wendell's eyes took on a thoughtful look. "That isn't my side of the business."

"Side?"

"Yeah. I booked the legitimate entertainment groups."

I crinkled up one side of my face. "I don't understand."

Wendell took another big drink. "Normally I wouldn't discuss my business like this, but..." He glanced around the room. "Considering the people here, I imagine my business, or at least that side of it, is the least offensive here."

I followed the guy's eyes and they landed on Bart who was talking with a rather sleazy looking man. The guy's dress wasn't what made him sleazy looking. His suit had to be very expensive, but on him it looked cheap. It was his mannerisms that gave him the sleazy appearance. I pegged him immediately as a drug dealer. My eyes went back to Wendell.

Wendell was watching me. "Since you know Hessor... What do you want to know about Ruth? But remember, this isn't my side of the business."

"What *is* your business and the *other side* of it?"

"I book singers, comedians, rock groups, celebrities, etc. If you have a function that you need a speaker, for instance, you contact me. I find the right speaker to present to your group. I get paid a fee by you."

"You're the middleman so to speak."

"Yes."

"And the other side?"

Wendell hesitated. "It was run by my partner. I am currently searching for a new one."

"Oh? Why?"

Wendell shrugged off the question. "He was in charge of the- How do I say this? The 'not so legal side' of the entertainment business."

"Uh? What did he do?"

"Hmmm... If you had a bachelor party, say, he would 'hire' the entertainers for you. As part of the fee, we would collect a percentage."

"Strippers?"

"Yes."

I rubbed my chin, looking off to side. "And Ruth Meddleson was one of your employees?" She was a singer, so it made sense, but if she was a singer then...

"Very much so. She was with us since the beginning, before I took over. Very reliable. Very dependable."

"What exactly did Ruth do? I know she sang."

"Singing?" Wendell chuckled. "You could call it that. And I might add, she was in great demand for *her singing*."

"Really? You make it sound like she did more than sing."

"She was a very talented *performer.*"

"A performer?" *No way. She was elderly. No way.* I shook my head.

"Very, very talented," Wendell qualified.

"But what did she do for you?"

Wendell's eyes looked at me like I was a very slow child. "She was an escort, you know."

"No, I don't know. An escort?" *Could she really be? Do elderly women do that?* "A prostitute? Really?"

Wendell chuckled at me and my naivety. "Yes. A high priced call girl, or should I say, woman."

I took a step back.

"Shocking, huh? I was shocked myself when I took over for... well, when I got into the business. She had quite the client list. Very loyal. Many of her clients she's had for years. A regular schedule she had until the last four months or so. Until then, she never gave us a bit of trouble."

I was pretty sure my mouth was still hanging open.

Wendell went on. "You'd be surprised how many guys like older women. I was fairly surprised myself. I would have imagined that the majority of men would want younger women. Not so. There is a huge market in older women. Very big market. And getting bigger all the time, especially as the demographics change. Even back before I came on board, older women were very marketable." He paused to drink. His posture changed as though he were lecturing.

"My theory is that although younger men like the 'game' of chasing a younger woman, they enjoy an older woman who knows what she likes, how she likes it and is not interested in head games. These older women, and I'm not just talking prostitutes here, are settled into their lives. They aren't looking for a husband. They want a good time. And, the younger man doesn't need to 'know' everything with an older woman. She'll teach him. Better yet, the older woman will tell him how to please her. And thereby, he learns too. Then there are those sick individuals that like Grannies." Wendell smiled. "Sick, but hey, everyone has his fetish."

"Ruth was one of your 'girls'?"

"Yes. As I said, a very dependable one. We'd give her an assignment, a client if you will, and we'd get nothing but good reports. A couple of the men even left her money when they died."

"What happened in the last four months?"

"I'm not really sure, to be honest with you. Maybe she was just tired of the business. I don't know. That was my partner's job. I only handled the legitimate acts."

"Any ideas? Guesses?"

"Well, I do know that her son was giving my partner a hard time. I'm not sure about what."

"Can I talk with your partner?"
Wendell drained the last of his drink. "Not likely."
"Why?"
"He's dead."
I was getting a bad feeling about this. "What was his name?"
"Cecil Weeks."

CHAPTER 14

Wendell moved back to the bar after I thanked him. The room was stuffy and I didn't want to really know what most of the people at the party did anyway. I headed out of the room to think. I was standing by the window looking at the dance floor when I felt a body move close to me, brushing my side.

"Problem?"

I glanced at Bart. "No, actually it's starting to make sense."

He watched me.

I looked away then back at him. "How much longer is this party going to take?"

"Had enough?"

"I don't want to know who any of those people are. You know how I feel about those things. How about if I just hang out here or in the club? When you're done, come find me."

"I suppose..." Bart's blue eyes were twinkling. "We could head to my private office."

My eyes met his. "Not likely."

"Sure? Or did Wendell offer you a position?" He was almost laughing.

I swung at him but he ducked. However, the second punch landed in his stomach. A whoosh of air escaped from his lips.

"I was only kidding," Bart managed to get out as he sucked in air.

My anger still thickened the air. I gave him a stare that made it clear that there would be 'no more'.

He stood upright and rubbed his stomach. "You're dangerous, Lady."

"Remember that."

He glanced around the back area. No one was near us at his booth and the other booths were secluded enough that no one had seen us. "Okay." He finally smiled. "Relax here." He motioned to the booth. "If you want a drink, ring the bell over there." He pointed at a small switch, nearly invisible against the paneling. "One of the waiters will come running."

I took a deep breath and exhaled it along with my anger.

Bart snuck in a quick kiss on the cheek. "Dangerous," he said as he walked away.

I spent the next hour watching the people on the dance floor. Crossing my arms, I started to get antsy. I'm not good at sitting and waiting for no reason. I should have followed Bart in my own vehicle so I could have left.

A movement caught my attention near the bar. A man's back looked familiar. My eyes panned back to the bar but he was gone. I frowned. I was so antsy that I was seeing things.

Enough of this.

I left the back area. I didn't need a waiter getting my drinks. Besides, I was too bored to sit any more.

After ordering a beer, I turned and surveyed the crowd. The music was still too loud. The people were loud too, laughing and shouting to each other. The lights were dimmer on the outskirts of the dance floor with the flashing lights working the main floor. The only regular light was here by the bar and even it wasn't that bright.

A hand tapped me on the shoulder. I turned to see the bartender smiling at me, holding out a micro-brew. I reached out of instinct for my back pocket where I always kept my money, not remembering that it was strapped to my ankle.

"It's on the house," he called over the music.

I grabbed the beer. "Are you sure?"

"Mr. Hessor pointed you out to us earlier. He said all of your drinks are on his tab. Enjoy, Ma'am." With a smile, he turned to another customer.

I frowned. Bart had pointed me out. I needed to stop this before he decided I was his girlfriend. *This would not do.*

Another hand landed on my shoulder. This one I recognized, I turned to find Bart sliding to my side. His arm draped across it in a very familiar way. His body right up against mine. Bart's eyes had a different kind of look to them, almost glassy. They were not his usual sharp eyes. I tried to step away but he held on tight. "I didn't find you at the booth."

Reaching up, I extracted his arm from my shoulder and backed away from him and the bar. Bart turned with a grin on his face to lean on the bar. I took another step back, opening my mouth to say something rude when I backed into a body.

I turned to apologize only to find myself staring into a very familiar face. John.

Shocked, I shifted away from him and collided with Bart who had stood up from the bar. My mouth was open as I looked from one face to the next.

"Hessor," John intoned.

Bart nodded with a glance at me. "Huddleston."

John turned the hard look and voice to me. "What are you doing here?"

"I uh, I uh… I was just leaving." I glanced back at Bart, who's eyes were now locked with John's eyes.

"Yes, you are," John said taking the beer out of my hand and forcefully setting it on the bar top. His other hand latched onto my arm. The grip squeezed hard. With a warning look at Bart, John began leaving, dragging me with him.

"Call," Bart yelled.

I peeked back to Bart then regained my composure. I yanked my arm out of John's grasp as we neared the door.

John put his hand on the small of my back, pushing me out the door. His hand stayed on me until we had moved a few steps from the building. He pointed down the street. The look on his face was as stony as Rich's when he fired me.

I stopped.

"Move." John's eyes flashed in anger as he stood between me and Rascals.

"Shove it up your-"

John grabbed my arm again, pulling me along.

"Let go." My anger began to boil. Much more of this heavy handed stuff and I would lay into John. Or, at least, I would try.

He let go but stayed one step behind me. His body was rigid. He was not taking 'no', or anything else I wanted to say, for an answer. We walked around the block and into a parking lot. He pointed down a row of cars.

As we neared the car, the alarm beeped off and I jumped in the car. I crossed my arms and sat there.

John started the car and drove off. The tension was a wall between us. It was as thick as if someone had actually built it with stone.

I didn't look his way, but I knew he was boiling mad. His face, immovable. His grip, wheel-crushing. His body, taunt. This was bad. I had never seen him mad before. It was scary. Not that I'd let him know that.

John drove until we left town. Once we reached a deserted section of the highway, he pulled over to the side of the road. Glaring.

I didn't acknowledge him in any way. I crossed my arms, tapping my left hand on the side of my body. Finally I couldn't stand the glare. I turned to him. "What?"

His eyes hardened more, if that were possible.

"I was-"

John's cell phone interrupted me. He let it ring again before looking at it. His eyes lifted back to mine as he opened it. "Yeah? No Rich, I don't know where Mel is." John's eyes were boring into my soul.

I swallowed, or at least tried. This was bad. Bad with all capitals, I'M IN BIG TROUBLE.

"I'm sure she's fine, Rich. You know she can take care of herself." John's eyes never left my face. "Is Roma calmed down?... I'm on my way back to town. Stop worrying... Yeah. Good." John hung up.

"Roma?" I asked, hoping to change subjects.

"You *will* call Rich when we finish," John said in a soft, yet authoritarian tone.

"Why was he trying to reach me?"

"Roma's having problems." John put the car in gear and took off.

"What kind of problems?"

"After we talk," John said. His voice was soft and low. This was a scary part of John I never wanted to see. "Tell me about tonight."

"I uh, I uh…"

John glanced at me, a sharp eagle-eye look.

I swallowed again. "I needed- I wanted to find out about Punky and…"

John's head snapped to me again.

"Don't say it. I know. We're off the case." I re-crossed my arms.

"Go on."

"Since Rich fired me, I didn't have access to the data bases. And this sort of information isn't in the data bases anyway."

"Dumb."

"Okay, not my smartest move-" I started to admit.

"Idiotic. Moronic. Unprofessional."

"I get the point, John." I brought my hands back down to my lap. "But I did find out-"

"He's nothing but trouble."

"Yes, I know. I was only using him-"

"You do know what he does for a living, right?" The sarcasm was deeper than universe.

"Yes. I was only-"

"Do you know what Rich would say?"

"Would you listen to me!" I didn't wait for a response. "I know all about Bart. And I knew he had connections that could get me the information fast. Simon didn't kill his mom. He has a plea bargain on the table for Monday, so I had to work quickly. Bart was the only way."

John's focus was on the road. His eyes squinted against the dark. His lips pressed tight. His face rigid. I had no idea what this silence meant.

"Simon didn't kill his mom."

"You have proof?" His tone had not changed at all.

"Well, no." I saw his head snap in my direction again, mouth ready to spit out some new word about my stupid actions. "He killed someone else that night."

John closed his mouth, skidding the car to the side of the road. He put the car in park and stared at me to continue.

"Simon murdered a guy by the name of Cecil Weeks…" John was nodding as though he knew the guy or at least knew of him. "And I think I might know why. Anyway, Simon was killing Buddy at the same time that someone else was killing Ruth." I gestured back to St. Louis. "He was here. Punky confirmed it. They both independently told me about Buddy being dead."

John looked off into the distance. I couldn't tell if he was still mad or not. "Why?"

"I'm not sure why. I can guess." I fiddled with the hem of my top. "Ruth was a prostitute."

John turned to me, slowly. His eyes narrowed to slits. His chin tilted higher as his frown increased, pursing to disapproval.

I nodded to emphasize my words. "Yeah. I found a whole bunch of costumes and stuff in her closet-"

"How did you get into-" John began.

I smiled. "Connections. I also talked to Wendell of Entertainment Extravaganza-"

John's eyes bugged out. "Do you know who he is?"

I shook my head.

A curse word escaped John's mouth. "He's connected to one of the biggest mobs in the country. His company runs over half of the high price call girls in St. Louis and the surrounding area. Stupid." John shook his head. "Stupid."

I looked at my shoes. And I all but insulted Wendell. I closed my eyes. It was over. Good thing I hadn't known that before the interview. I opened my eyes with a shrug. "He told me that Ruth was one of their best women. He explained a little about the industry. And he said that up until the last four months she was very dependable. He thought she might have been getting tired of the trade."

John was still shaking his head at me as though I was the world's slowest child.

"Ruth was HIV positive."

"What? How?-"

"I found a letter in her house and pilfered it."

John narrowed his eyes.

"I called the clinic using the anonymous number."

"Probably from a client," John intoned. He shook his head. "That still doesn't absolve you from your actions, Mel. We're off the case."

"I was fired. I no longer work for you."

"Not true," John said. His eyes once more resembling granite. "I wouldn't let Rich fire you. You're suspended until you come to your senses. But after tonight, I might fire you."

I was stunned into silence.

"Dumb. For as smart as you are, you are incredibly dumb." John put the car in gear and took off again. He shook his head once, mumbling to himself.

"Okay, I admit it's not one of my smarter moves-"

"Mel, shut up and listen. You will not see Hessor again. You will not get messed up in his business. Even the appearance of that is bad for our business. You are off the case right now, or you are permanently out of a job. Got it?"

"Look John-"

"No. You're like a little sister. I like you. I don't want to see you get hurt. Leave Hessor alone. Rich says you like to play with fire. Hessor will incinerate you."

"John-"

"I won't tolerate you acting like an immature school girl over a bad boy. You're not an adolescent." He was getting worked up now.

"Don't tell me what to do."

John swerved to the side of the road. He threw the car in park and leaned close. "Hessor is out of your life. Now."

My face reddened. The anger welled inside of me, searing its way to the surface. "You're right, I'm not a child. I can take care of myself. I don't need you or Rich, Mom or anyone else running my life. So just get off your high horse and-"

John's hand clamped on my mouth, hard. His face was inches from mine. His eyes like a black hole. His voice whispered hard. "Your anger doesn't scare me. Let me state it again. Hessor is out of your life."

I stared into his eyes. His hand was tight but he wasn't hurting me. It was his eyes that scared me. Intense, dark, deep, soul reading eyes. I was intimidated to say the least. But I was not going to be bullied. Slowly, I lifted my hand and pried his fingers off of my face.

"He was never in my life."

John didn't move.

"I was using him. He was using me, but I made it clear to him that I want nothing to do with him."

John relaxed a bit. His eyes still wary. "Why did he approach you like that?"

"I think Bart must have done some drugs after I left the party. I left the back area-"

"You were in the VIP area with him?!"

"That's where I talked Punky and Wendell. Before I left the area, about an hour before, I punched him in the gut because he proposed we go to his private office. He knows where I stand, John. I don't want him as a friend, let alone a boyfriend. I know him. I know how he operates."

John's eyes didn't waver.

"I needed the information. I saw no other way to get it. It was dumb. I admit that, but I got it and no one got hurt."

"Yet." His eyes flashed a warning.

I gave him a slight smile. "Scary."

"Good."

"So, are we still friends?"

John didn't answer but pulled away from shoulder, again. He settled back into driving. There was still tension in the car, but it wasn't high wire tension.

After a half hour of this, I cleared my throat. "So, what's up with Roma?"

John glanced at me. It was some time before he spoke. "Devon has upped the stakes."

"What?"

"He broke her front window last night."

"How?"

"A brick. Tonight, he knocked on her door, then, when she looked out the peep, he killed a cat."

"On her doorstep?"

"As she watched. The cops are trying hard to find him, but he's more slippery than snot." He shook his head. "Roma's scared to death. She told Rich she won't leave her house."

"I don't blame her," I said. *This is no way to live.* "Why did Rich want me?"

"We need your help."

I almost smiled.

"Don't get smug, Mel. The issue of Hessor is still in the forefront. I will not back down. He's a non-person for you."

"Got it. Trust me." I fiddled with my hem again. "What do you need?"

"We want to get Roma to a safe house. We're going to trick Devon."

"Trick him? How?"

"I'm going to sneak you into Roma's house, hopefully unnoticed by him. At the same time, I'm going to sneak Roma out. You'll pretend to be Roma for a day or two, so that we can get Roma someplace safe." He glanced at his watch.

I did the same. It was just after midnight.

"Maybe tonight." He paused in thought. "I'll drop you off at your home. Call Rich at the office. It'll only be two by the time we get this together. It should work."

I thought about it. Roma and I had about the same body shape. She was a little older than me and an inch or two taller. Our hair was similar in color. Her hair was longer but that could be covered up. It could work.

"One thing," I said looking at John. "Monday morning I'm scheduled to talk to Simon. I'll need to do that. Otherwise, I have nothing on my schedule."

John made a noise in his throat but said nothing else. The rest of the drive was in silence.

***

We sat in John's car, dressed completely in black, waiting on a phone call. We were waiting for Rich to tell us that all was clear. He was making a run through Roma's neighborhood paying special attention to the businesses down the block.

I touched the small bag of clothes between my legs, mentally checking off what I had hurriedly packed. *Yep, everything that I needed was there.* I glanced at John.

He seemed to be staring at nothing. His eyes twitched occasionally. He frowned once.

I cleared my throat to get his attention. When he looked at me, I inquired, "So, you've done something like this before?"

John gave a slight head nod. "Different reasons, similar operation."

"Where?"

John gave me a tiny grin. "I can't tell you that."

I smirked. "What? You'd have to kill me?"

"Nope. Just silence you." He made a motion of cutting my throat with his thumb. Finally, he smiled. "Small cut. Takes out your vocal cords. Yes, it was in the military, and no, I still can't tell you."

"How are we going to do this?"

"You follow me, in my footsteps. Stay quiet. Stop when I stop. Walk when I walk. Keep your ears and eyes open. Do not look directly at any object, look slightly off to the side. You can see things better that way in the dark."

"Yes, Kemosabe," I said as his phone rang.

He smiled. "Yeah?... We'll be in the house in fifteen minutes. Tell Roma not to turn on any lights and to leave her back door open. Make sure she's dressed in black, including her hair." He closed his phone as he looked at me. "Make sure your phone is off. We don't need an errant phone call messing this up." He checked his own phone. "Ready?"

I stuck the black stocking cap on my head and motioned him to lead the way. We got out of the car with me at his heels. I followed him the six blocks to Roma's house.

We stopped often, in dark recesses. John's eyes were busy checking things out. I felt secure with him, but I felt sort of foolish acting like this. We were directly behind Roma's house when a light in one of the apartments across the street flashed on.

John froze. I did the same and followed his gaze across the street to the apartment building.

There was a slight movement near the curtain but nothing else. The light went out. I glanced at John but he still hadn't moved. His eyes glued to the window. Slowly, he lowered himself to the ground. He made a motion that I took to mean that I was to imitate him.

I did. We stayed that way for what seemed like an eternity. My right leg started to twitch. The injury I had received in the car accident still bothered me, especially if I stressed it. This wasn't exactly stressing it, but I hadn't stayed squatted for this long since my accident. I looked again at John.

He glanced at me and slowly rose.

I followed stiffly.

His hand caught me by my upper-arm and helped me up. Then he moved extra slowly toward the back door. When we reached the back of the house, he paused again, checking out the houses behind Roma's. After only a short stop, we moved to the back door.

John opened the door and motioned me in. I tried to remember where her table was and stuff and was surprised that my eyes adjusted quickly in the dark. I moved away from the door and set my bag on the table. Catching a movement out of the corner of my eye, I jumped. Roma entered the kitchen.

The back door closed very quietly. "Are you ready to go?" John asked Roma softly, almost whispering.

Roma nodded. She was dressed in black except for her hair. "I don't have anything black for my-"

I handed her my stocking cap with a smile.

Roma smiled back as she put it on. She picked up her bag. "I made a list of things for you. It's on the counter here. Rich wanted me to write down what I usually do at night, my routine, so you could copy it as best as you can. It's here on the counter too. The fridge is stocked and, well..." She glanced at John.

His hand was on the doorknob waiting patiently.

I smiled at Roma. "I'll manage. Go. Be safe."

She smiled back and gave me a kiss on the cheek. "Be careful. He's dangerous."

I patted her on the back. "You too."

She moved toward John.

"Stop when I stop," John informed her. "Do what ever I do. It'll take us awhile to get back to the car." John glanced at me. "Call Rich and tell him you're in." He paused. "Do not open the door, Mel. You brought protection, right?"

I patted my bag. John and Roma left.

Looking around, I sighed softly and headed to her bedroom. I was sleeping tonight fully dressed and after a few minutes I finally got comfortable. I touched the object next to me. Reassured, I got comfortable. Lying next to me, as my constant companion now, was a Berretta.

My nine millimeter cuddly, best friend.

CHAPTER 15

I was in the hall bathroom brushing my teeth when the phone rang. I spit out the paste and moved into the kitchen to the listen to the answering machine. *Who would be calling this early?* I glanced at my watch. Six a.m. *Did Devon always start calling this early? No wonder Roma was forever tired, if he did this all the time-*

"Good morning, Roma. You're up earlier than normal."

I gasped. *How did he know I was up?* Roma had written that she never opened up her curtains and she never usually got out of bed before nine.

"I enjoy watching you get ready for bed, Roma. Pity I didn't see you actually sleeping. Did you enjoy the book last night?"

I grabbed my cell out of my pocket. "Rich, something weird is going on."

My brother yawned as he spoke, "What?"

"Devon just left a message that he knew I was up…" I relayed the rest of his message.

"What the- Roma thought someone might have broken into her house Friday. We looked around but didn't find anything missing. I wonder. Stay out of the bedroom. I'll be by to look things over. Roma said he was into... This is not good." I heard him moving.

"What?"

"Just stay away from the bedroom!"

"Okay, okay. Calm down. I'll stay away from the bedroom." I shut the phone with a huff. Rich was still mad at me, apparently.

It wasn't more than ten minutes and Rich was at the front door. I looked out the peep, then began to open all four of Roma's locks.

"Stay out of sight," Rich reminded me through the door.

"I know," I whispered to myself. *Did he think I was a complete moron?*

Rich walked in with just a quick look at me. "Stay here."

I gave Rich a disgusted look, but it was lost on him. He was already going to the bedroom. I stood in the hall listening to him move things in her room.

"Get me a stool or something."

I made a face. I looked in closets and rooms. Finally, I found a small step stool. I headed back toward the bedroom to meet Rich coming out. "This is all I could find."

The doorbell rang.

Rich grabbed my hand to hold me back. He passed me quickly. As he reached the door, he motioned me to stay out of sight. I did, making another face, this one Rich saw but chose to ignore. He checked out the peep. Then after just a glance at me, he opened it.

John walked in. "Anything?"

Rich nodded. "Found it in the ceiling. I just wanted you to confirm."

Both men moved toward the bedroom, neither acknowledging me. Rich grabbed the stool. I heard them talking in low tones in the bedroom.

Finally they walked out. Rich was already on his cell calling in the police. John stopped in the hall and stared to the side deep in thought.

"What did you find?"

Rich moved into the kitchen. John followed him. I tagged along. Rich sat as he spoke to Tom Hawkings. John leaned on the counter, arms crossed still deep in thought.

"What did you find?"

John ignored me again.

I stood in the middle of the room, waiting.

When Rich hung up he spoke to John, "Tom and two others will be here momentarily."

"Good."

I looked from one to the other. "What did you find?"

"This is not good," Rich intoned.

"He has to be nearby. It's a short range transmitter. He has to be within line of sight or at least there has to be a transmitter relaying the signal within visual range," John said looking at Rich.

I put my hands on my hips. "What did you find?"

Both men looked at me at the same time. Neither seemed inclined to answer me.

"Fine. Don't answer me."

John shifted on his feet. "We found a camera in the ceiling fixture. It looks like a recent installment."

I gasped. *Devon had watched me sleep!*

"It's not infrared," John said. "Just a standard camera. He probably turned it on this morning after you were up."

That did not make me feel much better.

The next hour police filled the house and I hid in the kitchen. Hawkings took the answering machine tape with him. They also took the camera after taking pictures of it and who knows what else they did. While they were working in the bedroom, John did a thorough search of the rest of the house. It didn't appear that there were any other cameras in the place.

After everyone left, John and I gathered in the kitchen again. I was drinking a soda at the table. John was checking out the phone lines to make sure they weren't bugged. Rich strolled in.

"Tom sent a squad to check out the businesses down the street, along with each car parked on the street. John, can you think of anywhere else the relay might be?"

John shook his head. "Puzzling."

Rich turned to me. "The bedroom is clean."

"I'll sleep on the couch anyway. There's no way I could sleep in there again tonight." I hesitated. "How long are we going to play this game?"

"Game?" Rich asked with a tone.

"Of hide and seek. Tomorrow, I have an appointment in the morning." I didn't even glance at John, but I knew he glanced at me.

Rich shrugged. "As soon as Roma calls me that she's safely at her destination, you can go. When is this appointment?"

"Before noon. Preferably earlier."

Rich nodded. "I think it'll work. She should be there by this afternoon."

"Where?"

"Oregon. We sent her to her parents under an assumed name and taking indirect flights. Her parents are going to hide her out at their house for two days. Then she'll fly into O'Hare and John will pick her up. We'll have some sort of safe place for her to go to."

"For how long?"

"Until we catch him."

"Could be a long time," I commented.

John shook his head. "He'll make another mistake. It was stupid to call and taunt Roma like that."

"Roma probably wouldn't have taken it the same way as Mel," Rich said. "Roma would've just been terrorized by the information. I doubt she'd have made the connection."

"Mel is sort of on the ball. Sometimes," John said looking at Rich.

Rich nodded, only gazing at John. "If she'd listen. Mel's so pig-headed. She gets a notion in her head and there's no beating it out of her."

"Has she been that way long?"

"All of her life. You should have seen her as a teen. Know-it-all-pigheaded. Hasn't changed one bit." Rich shook his head. "She'll be the death of me yet."

"Then beat some sense into her," John suggested.

I snorted.

"I tried. Didn't work; it only made her worse."

"What are we going to do?" John asked crossing his arms again.

"I don't know." Rich stood. "Unfortunately, she's actually pretty good at this. Go figure."

"Oh, so you do still love me." I smiled at Rich.

Rich smiled back. "Be careful. As soon as he figures out that we found the camera, he'll probably do something to retaliate."

I nodded.

"Probably tonight," John added. "We'll run by every twenty minutes or so. Call us at the first indication of trouble. And keep the gun handy."

***

Around three in the afternoon the phone calls began. He only left a message on the first one. "You found the camera." Devon laughed. "I'm disappointed. I think seeing you in your new purple nightgown would have been delicious. Oh, it's sitting on your front porch. Enjoy."

I hesitated then peeked out the peep. There was the package. *When had he done that? Why hadn't I heard him? Or the guys see him?*

I called Rich who called Hawkings. Through Rich, Hawkings ordered me not to open the door or touch the package. *Duh!* Shortly, Hawkings arrived to take possession of it. I thanked Tom through the door.

After that, the calls were irregularly placed. I got tired of it, so I shut off the ringer.

Rich called as the sun was setting. Roma was at her parent's house. John would pick me up in the morning. I was to dress in one of Roma's outfits and cover my face.

As I watched TV, I contemplated everything, but focused on Simon's case. I still couldn't think of another suspect. *And why make it look like Simon had done it? Who ever had framed Simon knew about him and his routine.* It was a puzzler. I wished more of the neighbors would talk to me. I knew I'd had missed something simple.

Neighbors.

With a quick flip, I opened the phone and called John. "Hey, why did it take Devon so long to figure out we found the camera?"

"Could be lots of reasons. Why?"

"Could the transmitter be like a voice dish thing?"

"A what?"

"You know those hand held, dish shaped thingies with the headphones, like they use at football games on TV. Point it at the area and pick up voices. But with video. Is that possible?"

John made a noise. "I don't know. Why?"

"What if Devon is a neighbor? Remember the light on in the apartment last night. Could he be living across the street?"

There was a long pause on the other line. "Very good thought, Mel. I'll look into it right now."

I smiled.

"Be alert, Mel."

"Always."

Around ten I heard a commotion on the street. I turned off the lights and peered out the window. Three squad cars, without lights, pulled up. The guys headed into the building across the street. Coordinated. Tense. Guns drawn.

After they disappeared into the building, I saw a figure walking toward the apartment building. He stiffened and stopped.

He wore a long coat and a ball cap that hid his face. He shifted twice on his feet as he glanced from squad car to building and back. Then his face whipped to look at me.

I knew him. Devon Miles.

I could feel his hatred from across the street. The hairs on my neck rose. My skin crawled. I swallowed.

Devon pointed at me then he disappeared. *How could he fade in the darkness like a wraith!*

I grabbed my phone and dialed John. Busy. Rich. Busy. A curse escaped.

Footsteps on the porch. My heart rate jumped into high gear. My hand shook as I grabbed the gun off the floor. A knock.

"Roma!"

Rich's voice. I exhaled and leaned my head against the wall. *Thank God.* With trembling legs, I stood. My arms were heavy as I stuck the gun in my waist band as I headed to the door. I took a deep breath as I opened it up. Rich jumped in.

"Why are the lights off?"

"I was watching. Devon saw the cops and got away."

Rich ran a hand through his hair. "Yeah. He wasn't home."

I could tell Rich was dead tired. I guided him into the kitchen and handed him a soda. "Where's John?"

Rich thumbed over his shoulder. "With the cops. You were right. He took the apartment the second day he was here." Rich shook his head. "Tom thinks that he also robbed two convenience stores. One in town and one in West Quincy. Must be where he got the money."

We sat in silence for a few minutes.

"What do we do now?"

"Same thing." Rich looked me in the eyes. "Be real careful. Now he's a cornered, dangerous animal."

I patted the gun.

Rich pointed at me, concern in his blue eyes. "Chest shot. Don't miss. Shoot to kill." Rich patted my hand still on the gun. "John and I will announce ourselves. Same with the police. Hawkings knows what we're doing."

"I doubt I'll sleep much tonight. Tomorrow's still the same?"

"John will call." Rich stood up. I walked him to the door.

Before leaving he stared at me. I knew he was still angry but it was softened with worry. He laid his hand on my shoulder.

"I'll be careful."

Rich smiled, gave me a hug then left.

The night dragged on and on. Every noise seemed amplified. Every creak grabbed my attention. I jumped at every new sound. Despite my anxiety, my eyes drooped and the couch became more comfortable.

A scraping noise sounded in the backyard. I listened but it didn't reoccur. I sighed. Either, it was my over-active imagination or some sort of animal. I wiggled.

I needed to pee. Even though I was comfortable, I knew the urge would only become more demanding. I hauled myself off the couch. Half way to the bathroom, I retraced my steps, grabbed my gun and cell phone from the coffee table. Better safe than sorry.

As I was doing my business the weak night light went out. *Was it just that light?* I tried the overhead light.

Nothing.

My heart went into over-drive.

I flipped the light switch off, redressed myself and slowly opened the door. Squatting down to make myself as small a target as possible, I hugged the wall, gun out and ready. I inched down the hallway. The doorway to the kitchen seemed like a black hole in front of me.

I listened.

Nothing.

Maybe there's a power outage in the whole area. Could I be that lucky? I halted. My ears strained to hear any noise. For once the whole house was strangely silent. I swallowed, trying to calm the gut tightening fear.

A scrape caught my attention. It came from the kitchen. I listened harder. It sounded like… like… the back door.

With my right hand gripping the nine millimeter tighter, I flipped open the phone with my left hand. My thumb searched for the redial button. I couldn't remember who I had called last, John or Rich. My eyes never wavered from the dark hole, the kitchen.

The seconds stretched out into minutes as I listened to the deafening ringing of the phone. Between rings I heard noises from the kitchen. They weren't as stealthy and whoever was making them, was working harder.

"Yeah?"

I inhaled when I heard John's calm voice. "Someone's at the back door. Power's off," I whispered.

"Stay quiet. Where are you?"

"Entrance to the hallway."

"Stay there. I'm only two blocks away. A patrol car will be there in seconds. Aim for the chest." The phone died on me.

I shook as I dropped the phone back into my pocket. My leg started throbbing from remaining squatted, but I ignored it. And I ignored its trembling. The rattle of the backdoor startled me.

There was a jangling on the outside, then it quiet.

I swallowed with a dry mouth, getting a better two-handed grip on the gun. Taking several deep breaths, I tried to calm down. I knew that if I shot like this, I would shoot wild. With each steady breath, slowly my heart rate dropped. Not back to normal, but it was no longer pounding in my ears. I loosened the grip on the gun. The gun felt heavy, its weight comforting.

The noise at the back door started again. A loud click. Silence. The pressure in the house changed. The back door was open.

I raised the gun. Steady. Calm. Ready.

One foot step in the kitchen. A pause. Another step. Another pause. Step. Pause.

My hair rose. My skin crawled. My gut twisted.

Step. Pause. Step. Longer pause.

Almost at the kitchen entrance to the hall. A slight shift of weight.

The silence echoed.

I re-gripped the gun. *Calm. Slow breaths. Chest shot. Aim to kill. Squeeze the trigger.*

Another tentative step.

CHAPTER 16

The footsteps retreated then vanished.

"Police, freeze!" Steve Wettle's voice.

"Backyard. He's heading- That way!" Hawking's voice.

I relaxed my grip a bit, then lowered the gun. Letting out a huge sigh, I laid the gun on the floor.

"Mel?" John called from the kitchen.

"Still in the hallway," I said lowering myself down to the floor. I stretched my throbbing, aching, twitching leg.

A flashlight turned on and came toward me. I leaned my head against the wall and closed my eyes. Another deep breath filled my empty lungs.

I opened my eyes as the light hit me.

John smiled as he squatted in the hallway. "You okay?"

I could only nod.

"They spotted him running out of the back door. There're four squads giving chase."

I nodded again.

John's smile grew. "He cut the power and phone lines."

"I figured."

John picked up the gun, disarmed it then stood. He held out his hand.

I took it and he lifted me off of the floor. I put my weight on the right leg, but it gave out. I would have fallen if John hadn't caught me.

"Are you okay?"

I shook my head, putting all of my weight on the left leg and rubbed the right one. "My right leg still gives me trouble. I over-stressed it. It'll be okay."

John helped me to the couch, concerned.

The door opened and Rich ran in. He stopped and released a relieved breath at seeing me. Then his face changed to apprehension, seeing me rubbing my leg. "Are you okay?"

"I was squatting. Hurt my leg."

Rich let out another breath.

"By the way," John said looking at me. "Great position you choose. Low and good view of the area."

I smiled. "Thank you, Dad."

It wasn't long before Tom Hawkings joined us. He did not look happy. "We lost him." He was a cop that anyone could pick out of a crowd; short hair, good build, reliable face, attitude of 'don't mess with me and back away'. "He's quick."

Rich and John exchanged looks.

Hawkings raked his hand through his hair. "We've got his description out on the radio and the state police are alerted. He took off in a dark colored pickup, probably a Chevy Tahoe." He looked at me. "Sorry."

I shrugged. *What could I say?*

Rich walked Hawkings out.

John turned to me. "Grab your stuff."

"What?"

"I'm taking you home."

"But, I thought…"

John helped me stand up. "He's not coming back here. The charade is over. Late Tuesday night, I pick Roma up at O'Hare. I have a place in Chicago ready."

I hurriedly gathered my few possessions. He didn't need to tell me twice.
***

I was shown into the jail's visitor room Monday morning. Viking had called at eight to tell me that Simon wanted to see me and that he had scheduled a meeting at ten. Viking also reminded me to talk to Simon about the plea bargain if I got there before him.

Simon was brought in. "You look whipped."

"Very."

"Anything?"

I looked Simon in the eyes. "I know you didn't kill your Mom."

Simon swallowed, but his beady little eyes stayed locked with mine. "Fine. Who killed Mom?"

"That I don't have an answer for." I paused. "Punky says to keep your bargain and he'll keep his."

Simon looked off to the side of the room. He sighed deeply. "Winnie?" His eyes rising to meet mine. "Find him?"

"No." I hesitated a beat. "Simon, did you do what you did in St. Louis because your Mom was HIV positive?"

Simon's eyes hardened. "That son of a... He forced her to…"

I waited.

His hands fiddled with the hand cuffs, then he suddenly sighed. "She was a good Mom. She provided for me. A lot of people would disapprove of her lifestyle. Well, she did her best." Tears formed in his eyes. "She was a good Mom."

I nodded.

"She didn't want to make that video, especially how he wanted it made. No protection. Mom was always so careful. That's how she got... Anyway, she wanted out. She was tired of... This guy... Mom got.... Buddy paid. I got him good."

"I'm sorry, Simon."

He shrugged. "Eye for an eye. I'll get less time on Mom's murder then I would on his. Besides, with his connections, I'd be dead. If I was here, I couldn't be there." Simon gave me a sad smile. "Mom to the rescue again."

The door opened and Viking walked in. Simon quickly composed himself.

Vincent sat. "It's now or we go to trial."

"Make the plea. I'll tell them anything they wanna hear." Simon stood. He held out his right hand to me, his left following suit tagged along by the cuffs. "Thanks, Mel. I owe you one." He turned to Viking as we both stood. "Out of Mom's estate before you invest it for me, pay Mel for her time. Whatever the going rate is, double it." He winked. "Guard!"

\#

There were three messages on my answering machine when I got home, Max, Roma, and one of the veterinary hospitals in Quincy. I took down the information from the last before I did anything. I rubbed my eyes and called Roma first.

"I just heard. Are you okay?"

I smiled. "I was never in any real danger, Roma. He only made it into your kitchen."

"Have they found him yet?"

"Unfortunately, no. I talked with Rich earlier. They think he's cleared the area. The police recovered the vehicle. It was in an accident outside of St. Louis. According to witnesses at the scene, he fled on foot." I yawned. I was going back to bed as soon as I made these calls.

Roma sighed. "I hope they catch him soon."

"Me too."

"I would've been so terrified. You're so brave." She sniffled. "You guys have really given me my life back. I'm hopeful that soon I can live a normal life again. Thank you so much, Mel."

I blinked back unexpected tears. It must be because I was so tired. "You're welcome. Just enjoy the time with your parents. And don't miss that flight to Chicago. John has a place for you to stay."

"Thanks again. I'll be at the airport with plenty of time to spare." She was smiling, I could tell. "I'm so happy."

I hung up with a smile on my face. Then I quickly dialed Max as I walked into the bedroom. The veterinarian call could wait until later or even tomorrow.

"Hello."

"Hi Max."

"Is something wrong?"

"No. Why?"

"You sound, different."

"Tired. I pulled an all-nighter."

Max chuckled. "And you thought private detective work would be all glamour."

I chuckled. He always made me feel so good. "Oh yeah. I thought I'd drive Ferraris and live on estates in exotic places like Hawaii."

"Are you saying Quincy isn't exciting?" Max asked with a smile in his voice.

"It has its moments."

***

Tuesday was clear but chilly. I had slept most of Monday afternoon. Rich called and told me to report to work today. I smiled as I finished eating my breakfast. I knew that blood was thicker than any petty dispute.

I was disappointed that I never found out who had killed Mrs. Meddleson, but at least I had been right. Simon didn't kill her. That made me feel better. That and the fact, that although Simon was going to prison, he wasn't totally innocent.

I spied my note about the vet call. I crumbled it up and threw it away. The case was closed. Winnie was probably dead.

Washing the dishes, I planned my day. My eyes strayed back to the garbage can. I dried my hands and pulled the paper out. I smoothed it on the counter as I picked up the phone. If I didn't call this person back, it would haunt me. *What if?* This way, the person would tell me 'no, I never saw a little Shih Tzu' and I would feel that I could let the case go. The entire case.

"I'm sorry he stepped out for the minute," a lady told me. "He'll be back in a minute. If it's about an animal, he's at the hospital right now. If you need something, you can just show up. He should be there for another half hour or so."

I hesitated. Dr. Helbring's office was located on the edge of town. He wasn't always open, but when he was, he did good work according to my sources. He'd been away on a 'family emergency' when I had originally called.

Yes, I would follow this up. For my peace of mind.

"That's what I'll do, thanks." I hung up the phone and grabbed my stuff. I could do this and make it to work. I glanced at my watch as I locked the apartment. *Okay, I might be a few minutes late. But what would Rich do, fire me?*

The hospital was a small building behind his house. I opened the door and walked to the counter. No one was around. I rang the bell. Still no one was answered.

I moved around the counter and checked out the three rooms behind it. Cats and dogs but no people.

"Hello?" I called out.

"Out here."

I followed the voice out the back door. An older man, probably in his late fifties, was checking a horse's leg.

Dr. Helbring looked at me and smiled. "I'll be with you in a minute."

"Take your time."

And he did. He and the owner of the horse were deep in consultation about the horse's leg. I was listening but they used too many technical terms for me to understand. All I got was that the horse was favoring the leg and this was bad.

Finally, the vet helped the horse back into the trailer and shut the gate. He reassured the guy that he'd visit later in the day to see the horse working out. The salt and pepper haired doctor walked over to me as the horse's owner drove away. "Now, how can I help you?"

"I called awhile ago about a Shih Tzu. Did you get the message?"

His face scrunched in puzzlement. "I'm sorry. I don't think I did. Were you the lady I called yesterday about the returned phone call?"

I nodded.

"The service wasn't real clear what you had wanted. A Shih Tzu?"

"Yeah, some time ago. A small Shih Tzu." I dug in my fanny pack for Winnie's picture.

Helbring took his glasses from his shirt pocket and put them on. He still held the picture at arms length as he studied it. Suddenly his face loosened up in recognition. "Oh right… Now I remember. Yeah, late one night. I got a knock on the door. A man hit a little dog. He wanted me to look at the dog." The doctor motioned me into the building handing me the picture.

My heart beating faster. Maybe I could clear *something* in this case.

"That could be the little dog."

"How badly was he hurt?"

"The dog?"

I nodded. I wanted to say 'no the man, silly' but that would be way too rude.

"Well…" Helbring rubbed his chin. "Let me pull the file." It took several minutes but finally he came up with it. "Bruises, cuts on his front legs. Big cut on his side. Poor little thing took a good hit to the head. Lost quite a bit of blood." He was shaking his head. "I remember him now. Cute little dog. I was afraid he wouldn't make it, but he pulled through."

My heart was beating faster. "Who brought him in?"

"A man."

"Can you describe him?"

The vet looked at me as though I was crazy. "I'm not good with people. That's why I work with animals." He seemed to be thinking anyway.

"How old?"

He shrugged.

I almost sighed. "Do you remember anything about his face?" I waited. He came up with nothing. "His hair color? Eyes? Scars? Anything?"

Helbring continued to think. "It was really late at night, I was half asleep. I focused on the dog. Sorry."

"Okay. What about the guy's address? Did he leave one?"

The doctor shook his head. "That's the funny thing. I had him filling out paperwork while I checked on the dog. He said he hit the little thing with his car. Such a little dog going up against a car, I was extremely worried." The doctor crossed his arms after pulling off his glasses. "I took the dog and went in to begin to work on him. The guy was supposed to fill out the paperwork and join me in the observation room." He motioned to the room we were in.

I looked around. There were small cages and several cats in them. One dog watching us. I turned back to the vet.

"When I figured out that the dog was going to live, I looked up and the guy was gone. I walked out to the counter..." He did the actions as though it was that night. "Here on the counter I found a note. It said to take care of him and find him a good home. On top of the note was a hundred dollar bill." The doctor shrugged.

"A hundred?"

He nodded. "I figured he felt bad about hitting the dog and didn't want to let anyone know about it. The next morning I called all around the area. No one owns a Shih Tzu around here."

"What happened to Winnie?"

"Who? Oh, the little Shih Tzu. Is he yours?"

"No." I almost sighed again. "Winnie belongs to a... a friend. What happen to him?"

"I know this little old lady who just lost her dog four months ago. Since no one claimed him, I gave him to her."

"Can I see the dog?"

"Uh... Are you going to take him away from her? The reason I ask, is because he seems to have settled in well with her and I-"

I stopped him with a hand motion and a smile. "The friend of mine was an older lady and she passed away. I just want to make sure that it's Winnie, so I'll feel better about everything. I've been so worried that he ran away and died."

Helbring let out a sigh. "Okay. Let me call her and let her know that you're coming over. Okay?"

"Sure." I glanced at my watch as he looked up this lady's number. I stepped outside and called Rich to tell him that I was running late. Luckily, Rich wasn't in yet. So I just left him a message. Pam sounded happy that I was coming back.

The doctor stepped outside. "Here's her address. I explained the situation to her. She's still worried that you're going to take Hercules away from her."

"Hercules?" I smiled. "No. I'm not. Thanks for all of your help." I handed him a card. "If you think of anything else about the man, please don't hesitate to call me." I hurried away.

The house was an old farm house stuck in the middle of a new subdivision. It probably belonged to the original owner of the land. I put on a smile as I rang her doorbell.

An elderly lady with a walker came to the door. She looked at me with a suspicious air.

"Mrs. Warbler, my name is Melissa Addison. I know the former owner of Hercules and I just want to make sure that it's him."

"That's what Warren said."

I nodded at her through the closed screen door. "The lady who used to own Hercules, if he's the right dog, is deceased. I've been searching for him afraid that he was dead. All I want to do is make sure it's him, for my own peace of mind." I smiled again. "I'm really worried about him. I hope Hercules is Winnie. It looks like he has a nice home with you."

That seemed to break down her defenses. She smiled at me finally, and let me in the house.

"I put him in my bedroom, so... well, my Shakespeare died a couple of months ago and I didn't want Herc to be taken away. I've gotten so attached to him." She slowly made her way through the living room. "Wait here."

I stood just inside the door.

Within seconds, the little 'mutt' came scooting into the room, barking and growling at me. He was a ferocious little dog. I squatted with the picture in hand. *Yep, it was Winnie.* Reaching out, I let Winnie, Hercules, sniff my hand. Slowly he calmed down and made nice with me. I looked up to see Mrs. Warbler watching us as I petted him.

"Is it him? Is he that other lady's dog?"

I gave her a sad nod as I stood. "Yeah, he is. And I know Ruth would want you to keep him. I'm sure she would be happy that you could provide such a nice home for him. He looks as though he really loves you too." Hercules had moved back to her side and was sitting there wagging his tail.

She looked down. "What was his name?"

"It was Winston, Winnie for short. But I think Hercules is a better name. He thinks he's so much more dog than his size."

Warbler laughed. "That he does. And I promise he will always be loved here."

I smiled. "Thank you for letting me put my mind at rest, Mrs. Warbler."

"You're welcome dear."

After getting into the office and finding that Rich had left me a pile of employee searches to do, I called up Vincent Viking.

"Yes, Mel?"

"Could you relay a message to Simon for me?"

"Sure."

"Tell him I found Winnie. He's fine and in a loving home. He has one scar on his leg but other than that he appears okay." I was smiling. At least, I had done that for Simon.

"That should make him happy. By the way, the plea bargain went through. I want to thank you for your help, Mel."

"Sure."

"Did you want me to send the money to the office or your home address?"

"Better make it my home." I was glad he had asked. That's all I needed was for Rich to find out that Simon had paid me.

I settled into the morning routine. It was nearing lunch time when Pam called that I had a phone call.

"This is Warren Helbring, from the vet hospital this morning."

"Yes, Dr. Helbring?"

"I did remember one thing about the guy. Ever since you left it's been bothering me that I can't remember him. I still don't remember too much about him, except his hands. They were strong hands, you know, like he did a lot of work with them even though he was as old as me or older. And he had really bushy eyebrows."

I frowned. "Okay."

"I hoped that helps."

"It might. Thanks for calling." I hung up and shook my head. With a shrug, I went back to typing but after several key strokes I stopped.

Bushy eyebrows. Strong hands.

Earl Boden.

CHAPTER 17

I dialed his number with a trembling hand. I bet he had visited Ruth and had found Winnie after he had been hurt. So, without incriminating himself, he took Winnie away.

There was no answer.

I set the phone down slowly. Thinking hard. I picked up the phone again and dug into my notes on the desk for Stella Beaverton's number.

"Mrs. Beaverton, is Mr. Boden back yet?"

"Yes, Earl got home yesterday late afternoon and came by to see me. He was very happy to be home, I think. He brought me over a statue of his that I have always loved. Funny, he gave Eugenia something too. He must be in one of his gift moods. We spent the night just cuddling. He seemed sad but he didn't want to... well, you know. He gave me a kiss on the cheek and told me to be good." She giggled.

"Be good?"

"He always says that when he's going out of town or something."

"Is he home right now?"

"I would think so."

"Thanks." I hung up and dialed Boden's number again. "Come on, Earl..." I pleaded to the ringing phone.

"Yes?" The voice sounded tired, old, or defeated. Not like the Earl Boden I knew.

"Mr. Boden?"

"Who is this?" It sounded like he really didn't care.

"Mel Addison." I hesitated. He sounded really different. "Are you okay?"

"No. I'm in hell. I'm going to hell."

"What?"

"It doesn't matter."

There was a noise on the other side of the line, as though the phone was dropped. "Mr. Boden... Mr. Boden... Earl!" I strained to hear anything on the line. I could hear what sounded like movement but nothing else. Then Scruffy barked. I dropped the phone on the hook and ran for the door.

***

I pounded on Mr. Boden's door, calling to him. I heard Scruffy barking on the other side. I tried the back door. Then I ran back to the front, trying to look through windows. The shades were pulled. I rang the bell again then banged on the door.

"Go away."

"I want to help, Mr. Boden. I know you took care of Winnie. I found him." I cursed softly under my breath trying to see something, anything inside through the blinds.

"Is he okay?"

"He's fine and the vet found him a good home. Mr. Boden, did you see who killed Ruth?"

"Yes." His voice sounded distracted.

"Why didn't you say anything?"

"I can't."

"Who did it, Earl?" I shouted through the door.

"I did."

I stood back from the door and scrunched up my face. It fit. It did. "Why?"

"Ruth had AIDS."

"Yes, she was HIV positive. I know. But it's not contagious unless-" I stopped. *Earl was having a relationship with Ruth too?* I swallowed hard. "Did she... Are you-"

"And now I have it too. How can I continue to see my other girls?" A sob came from the other side of the door. "How do I tell them they need to get tested for this horrible disease? That I might have killed them too."

"Just because you're HIV positive doesn't mean-"

"I got it from her. She gave me this- I didn't know she was a whore. She told me... I thought she just got it from her lover. She told me she was seeing someone else. I thought, I thought it was just one other guy. That would have been okay-" He voice broke. "Then she told me to go to the doctor and get tested." Another sob. "I... I... My life is ruined. I can't live like this. I didn't mean to hurt her. When Ruth... when she told me I... she told me she was a... That she got it on... One of the movies she made. I... I hit her. I hit her and she fell. There was so much blood. She wouldn't stop bleeding. The next thing I knew she was dead... I saw my hands around her neck... Winnie was biting my leg. I hit him, knocking him across the room. I thought I'd killed him too.... I cleaned up.... Then it hit me, I can't go on... I just can't... Mel?"

"Yeah? Open the door, Earl!"

"Take care of Scruffy."

The gun shot reverberated through me like I had been hit. I stumbled backwards.

"No!" I grabbed my cell and dial 911. "Earl!"

I could still hear Scruffy barking. Suddenly, the barking changed to a whine. "Earl!" I began to beat on the door again.

After giving the information to the 911 operator, I continued trying to get into Boden's house, but it was locked up like a fortress. I ran back to the front porch. I could still hear Scruffy whining but nothing else. Except sirens. Approaching fast.

Still pounding on the door, I was shoved off to the side, strong arms holding me pressed up against the house. Mitch. Gun drawn. Tense.

"Shots fired? You okay?"

"I said *shot* fired. Mr. Boden shot himself, I think. Help him." I motioned to the door. Steve Wettle was hunched on the other side of the doorway, listening intently for sounds from the house and to us.

"Anyone else in the house?" Mitch asked, as he released me from the wall.

"Not that I know of. You've got to get in there. Please hurry, Mitch!"

The two cops exchanged a look. Steve shook his head. Mitch glanced at me then looked back at Steve. Something was communicated because Steve grimaced then retreated to the squad as more sirens approached.

Mitch glared into my eyes. "Stay here. Don't leave this spot until we've cleared the house. Got it?"

I nodded briefly at Steve rejoined us on the porch with a small battering ram in hand. Two more squads cars screeched to a halt. Car doors flung open. Cops advancing; guns in hand.

"Stay." Mitch ordered one more time, then nodded at Steve. With one colossal slam, the door imploded, splintering its frame. Cops swarmed in the house, guns drawn.

"Clear... Gun secured."

"He's still alive... Get paramedics."

"Clear."

"Clear." The various cop's voices floated out to me.

I peeked around the door frame to find the room empty. Except for Earl on the floor. The pool of blood spreading around him. The smell of gun powder hung in the air along with fresh blood smell. Scruffy stood guard near the body, barking at everyone.

I hurried in and scooped him up. Moving off to the side as the cops filed back in, I watched the gruesome scene unfolding before me. Finally, Scruffy laid his head on my arm and whimpered. Instinctively, I cuddled him closer.

Mitch felt for a pulse. He looked up at me. "What's his name again?"

"Earl Boden."

Mitch stood and shuffled me out onto the porch. "I told you to stay outside. Why are you in here?"

"I called and he sounded strange. I was worried. He was talking strange. He has been acting sort of weird with his friends in the neighborhood the past couple of days. I was worried." I looked at Mitch as tears gathered in my eyes. "I just had a feeling. He... I called when I heard the gunshot."

Mitch shook his head. "I wonder why he was so despondent?"

I looked at my feet as hot tears streaked down my face.

"Did he say anything to you, Mel?"

"He was just tired of it all. He said he couldn't go on."

Mitch just shook his head as the ambulance pulled up.

"Will he make it?"

Mitch glanced back into the living room as the medics hurried into the house. "I don't know. With some of these suicides, the way he did it-Sometimes they only manage to do a lot of damage. Do you know if he had a next of kin?"

"I know he has a daughter in Chicago. I can get you her number from one of the ladies here on the block."

Mitch nodded. "Stay here on the porch, Mel. I'll have Steve take your statement." He disappeared into the house then walked back out following the paramedics as they wheeled Earl, his head bandaged, to the ambulance. Mitch stopped next to me. "Are you okay?"

I watched them all the way to the ambulance. Mitch placed an arm around my shoulder and hugged me. "Are you okay?" His blue eyes filled with concern.

I nodded. "Mrs. Beaverton will know his daughter's number."

"Give Steve the information. One of us will contact her. Sit down on the swing. You're ghost white." Mitch escorted me to the swing on Boden's porch. "I called Rich. He's on his way."

Scruffy gave out a soft whine as Mitch walked over to his cruiser to retrieve something. I hugged the little poodle closer and gently stroked his head. I gave him a little kiss on the head as the ambulance drove off. "It's okay, Scruffy."

#

Less than an hour later, I left Boden's house. Rich wanted to drive me but I assured Rich and Mitch that I was okay. I asked Mitch if I could take Scruffy with me. I didn't want him going to the pound tonight. Mitch patted my arm and sent me on my way.

Scruffy was lethargic. He just let me hold him and pet him. The toy poodle had a glazed look to his eyes. I felt bad for him. *He is so old. Would he survive the pound?* I certainly couldn't keep him. I stroked his head as he lay in my lap.

A sudden thought popped into my head. I started the Jeep and drove several blocks away. I stopped in front of the Allen's house. *Maybe...*

Frank Allen met me at the door. His eyes were red and blood shot. I could hear Mary Alice crying. I knew that the cops had already interviewed the various neighbors, especially the Allens, Beaverton and Hamilton. He motioned me in.

"Uh..." I didn't know how to ask this. "I found Winnie. He's fine and in a good home. But until Mr. Boden recovers or..." I didn't want to say died.

Mary Allen nodded still crying. Frank held out his arms for the poodle. "Scruffy can stay with us."

I handed the little dog to him. "Thanks, Mr. and Mrs. Allen."

"It's the least we could do," Frank said petting and cuddling the dog. "The police said you were there."

"I tried to get him to open the door."

"Do you know why he did it?" Frank asked with a sniffle.

I shook my head. "He was talking nonsense." There was no need to tell the truth, it would help no one. Unless Boden survived. Then I would go to the police with my suspicions and what he said. My statement to Steve had been vague, leaving open that possibility.

"I wish we had known he was so depressed. He seemed fine the last time I talked to him. If we had only known," Frank said. "Earl was always the rock of the neighborhood. I mean, when Mary had her stroke, he was so helpful."

"He's a good neighbor," I said with a pat on his arm.

Mr. Allen looked up at me from Scruffy. He was gently stroking the limp poodle. "Do you know his condition? Will he survive?"

I sighed, blinking back tears. "I don't think it looks good. The emergency room doctor told my brother, one of the cops at the scene, that he thinks Mr. Boden did just enough damage to make him unresponsive. He doesn't think he'll die unless complications set in, but they're still in surgery. There'll be more tests after surgery too, but the ER doctor didn't sound very hopeful."

"So he'll get better?" Mary asked wiping her face with a tissue.

I shook my head. "The ER doctor says probably not. He'll be uncommunicative."

Frank frowned. "A vegetable?"

I shrugged. "They don't know for sure."

"His worst fear. He always said he wanted to die, not be hooked up to a machine and just lie there."

I looked at the floor.

"Will he know where he is and stuff? Can he or will he be able to know people if they come to visit?" Mary asked.

"I don't know. I'm sorry." I gave Scruffy one last, gentle pat on the head and a scratch behind the ears. "If you need anything, don't hesitate to call. And someone should check up on Mrs. Beaverton and Mrs. Hamilton. I know they took it hard."

Frank walked me to the door. "Thanks, we will."

I drove off still fighting the tears. Well, not the way I expected this case to go. I was stunned as I headed into the office. When I entered, Rich was in the front area.

He motioned me back to his office and shut the door. He gave me a hug. "Okay?"

I swallowed back my tears. "Yeah."

"Are you sure?"

"Yeah but you'd better sit down."

His eyebrows furrowed in puzzlement, but he sat anyway. "What?"

"I know who killed Ruth Meddleson."

His face hardened momentarily, then softened. "Go on."

I took a deep breath and wiped at my wet eyes. "Simon's innocent. He was killing a guy by the name of Cecil Weeks in St. Louis at the same time that someone was killing Ruth Meddleson."

Rich narrowed his eyes.

"Earl Boden killed Ruth Meddleson. He told me before he shot himself. Ruth was a prostitute. She got HIV, according to Simon, on one of her last 'assignments' for her boss, Cecil Weeks. Simon said she was forced to do it."

"Simon knew this?"

I nodded. "That's why he killed Weeks. Ruth found out she was HIV positive and told Boden to get checked."

"Why him?"

I smiled sadly. "Earl was the neighborhood stud. Anyway, he said he was HIV positive too. In a fit of passion, when Ruth told him…" I drifted off not finishing the statement.

Rich leaned back and thought about all I'd told him. "How did you piece it together?"

"Earl told me through the door before he tried to off himself. Winnie was the key. Earl couldn't hurt Winnie, especially after he came to his senses after killing Ruth."

Rich was nodding. "He took him to a veterinarian."

"Yep."

Rich's gaze fell on me. "What are you going to do with the information?"

"I don't know." I shrugged. "I'm asking you. You're the professional here. Simon has already plea-bargained with the DA. So if he was here-"

"He couldn't be in St. Louis killing Weeks," Rich finished for me. "Smart move. He'll probably get less time here than there. Smart."

"Boden's in his own living hell."

"Didn't do the job right?"

I shook my head. "Still alive but beyond that…" I shrugged. "So, no one knows what I know and there's no way to confirm it."

Rich shook his head. "Bad."

"Do I go to Hawkings with the information?"

There was no answer.

"I mean, everything's settled. Everyone is happy. Do I rock the boat with unverifiable evidence?"

Rich didn't answer for a long while. "What to do?" he whispered then he looked at me. "It's up to you, but there really isn't much they can do about it."

"What about the old ladies? Do I tell them to go get checked? I mean if Earl was infected, he could have given it to them."

"Did they use protection?"

"I don't want to know." I shuddered.

Our eyes met.

"Mel, it's your choice." He leaned forward in his chair. "I'll support you in whatever you decide."

"I need to think about it." I stood. "I'm heading home."

CHAPTER 18

I was microwaving food for supper when I saw Dad's car parking in the lot behind the Full Moon. I frowned when I noticed Mom was with him. *Great. Just great.*

I had already talked with Mom on the phone, twice. Now she was here. I sighed as I heard the hurried footsteps on the stairs to my apartment. I clenched my fist then released it. *I can do this. I can get through this. Keep thinking of...*

"Mel?" Mom called through the screen.

I stepped closer so she could see me. "Hi. You didn't need to come by."

"Nonsense." She opened the door and stepped in followed by Dad who flashed me an 'I'm sorry' look. "We were out doing our monthly Shut-In Visits for the church." She gently stroked my arm. "Are you doing okay still? Do you want to talk about your day?"

"I'm fine." I gave her a smile. Maybe *if she sees me acting normal she'll leave.* "Really. And I've talked about it to about everyone, the cops, Mitch, Rich, John and even Pam." *Here I go lying again.* "I'm sad, but really, go visit the old folks. They enjoy it when you visit." I patted her back on the arm.

"Are you sure, because we can stay here and help. Do you have- I see that you're eating. Good."

Dad shook his head in frustration behind her back. He looked deeply into my eyes. Catching his eye, I nodded. I was okay.

"Okay, well Dot, we'd better get going then. Mr. Timberman always needs to be reminded to take his medication." He reached for Mom's arm. Mom hesitated, searching my face. She held her ground as her eyes narrowed.

I gave her arm another pat. "Go. I'll call if I need anything. I promise."

Mom leaned in and gave me a kiss then a quick hug. "Well. I guess."

Dad motioned her to the door. After she left, he turned to me and lowered his voice, "Take it slow. Call Mitch or me."

"Thanks."

He winked and left.

With a sigh, I grabbed my supper and headed to the couch. But I didn't feel much like eating. *What am I going to do?* I had pretty much decided that I wasn't going to tell Hawkings. The information would do more harm than good.

But what about the ladies? Both were in their late sixties or early seventies. Would it be worth having them get upset over something that might never happen? And even if they did get infected, would it matter? I sighed.

The phone rang pulling me from my reverie and I stood to grab the portable but didn't answer the phone.

"Hey Mel. I guess you aren't home..." It was Max on the answering machine. "I was calling because I was bored..."

I still didn't want to talk, but his voice made me feel warm. I suddenly needed, no wanted, a sympathetic ear. I knew I could tell Max anything and he would listen and help. He was a good friend. I took a deep breath as I turned on the phone. "I'm here."

"Hey, are you okay? What's the matter?"

"Nothing."

"Can't pull that with me again, Tiger. I can tell something's wrong. Want to talk about it?"

"No."

There was a momentary pause. "Okay. So, how's the weather there?"

I smiled. "I said I didn't want to talk about it."

"I just asked about the weather."

"Bauer, you're so transparent."

Max chuckled. "Well then, talk to me."

"I found the dog and who killed the old lady. And the guy who did it tried to kill himself. It was awful. He wanted to talk before, I think. I guess he just wanted to confess it to someone, but he didn't do it right though."

There was a long pause as Max obviously tried to adsorb what I had said. "Did he try to kill himself in front of you?"

"Sort of."

"Mel?"

"I was on the other side of his front door. What do I do?" I rubbed my eyes as the tears started again. "I don't want to tell these old ladies and ruin their lives."

"Ruin their lives? What are you talking about? Start at the beginning, Mel. Tell me what happened." His voice was gentle and comforting.

I told him about the HIV thing and Earl and about Ruth's job. I left out the part about Simon and Weeks.

"That's a tough one," Max said, "but I think you've already decided though."

"Yeah. I just need to work up the courage."

"Wish I could help you."

"You just did." I smiled at the phone. "Thanks."

"That's what friends are for. Now…" His voice changed. "Care to come out to visit me?"

"Bauer, I hope you never change." I chuckled.

"I'm glad you're feeling better."

"Yeah. Thanks." I smiled through a sniffle.

"Mel?"

I tried to blink back the tears but it was useless. "Yeah?"

"Are you crying? Why?"

"I don't know." I sniffled again, wiping my face as the tears flowed down my cheeks. "Life. Death. It's so sad." I hugged myself, slightly rocking. "I miss Robbie."

There was silence on the other end. Softly Max spoke, "I wish I could give you a hug, Mel."

I smiled through my tears.

"Mel? Are you still there?"

"Yeah." I suddenly felt a lot better. "Thanks for talking with me, Max. I appreciate it. And you have hugged me. I've never gotten such a nice voice-hug ever."

Max chuckled. "I aim to please."

I talked with Max for half an hour longer about other things. He always cheered me up when I was feeling down. As I was eating, the phone rang again.

"I've got news for you," said Mitch.

"Oh yeah?"

"Rich called. Asked if there was any way we could get Boden tested for HIV. Lots of holes in his story of why, but, anyway, I asked the doc. They did on the condition that I told no one. He's not infected."

"What? He told me he was HIV positive."

"The ER doc said that most men his age probably wouldn't have gotten tested. He knew Boden tangentially through some gardening club or something." Mitch chewed on something then continued. "Hated doctors with a passion after his wife died. Said he had no use for them. He was pleasant to the ER doc when they talked about gardening but once he mentioned his heart condition and was mad when the doc started questioning him. Also the doc said that Boden was fast to jump to conclusions. So he probably just thought he had the virus."

"Oh man! He thought-"

"Yeah, that's what Rich said."

I collapsed on the stool. Taking a deep breath, I tapped my finger on the counter. "Well, at least the other ladies don't have to worry now."

"Did you tell them yet?"

"No, I was going to head over there tonight, but..."

"Yeah, enough lives have already been turned upside down by his actions."

"How is he?"

"He has no higher functions. The brain scans show that his basal stem is working but there's no other brain activity."

"So, he's a vegetable."

"Yep."

"Such a waste."

"Yep."

"How's the investigation going?"

"It's been ruled a botched suicide. The daughter's on her way down here, but he'll probably spend the rest of his natural life in a nursing home just laying there."

"One of his neighbors said he didn't want to be kept alive with machines."

"That's up to his daughter now."

I rubbed my face.

"Are you okay, WT?" Mitch was the only one that still called me that from our teenage days. 'Wild Thing' accurately described those times.

"Yeah, thanks for asking. Max called earlier and he cheered me up."

"Good. Well, I gotta go. Tina and I are heading out to a movie. Want to join us?"

"No thanks. Three's definitely a crowd. Gonna rope this one in, cowboy?"

Mitch chuckled slightly. His voice took on a western accent, "Well, she is the best heifer in the herd that I've seen so far. I don't know yet. Gotta spend a little more time, you know testing her out first. Thank ya little lady for the thought. I best be going. See ya'all."

I chuckled as I hung up the phone. A burden seemed to have been lifted, but I still felt depressed. Earl had ruined too many lives, including his own, but at least I hadn't had to upset the two old ladies with more bad news.

I rocked Petey and myself to sleep that night.

***

Wednesday morning when I showed up at work, Rich was on the phone. He was upset about something. Rich pointed to the chair in front of his desk.

I sat.

"Okay. I will... Yeah, just give us a call if we can do anything, Mr. Tronloski... Absolutely. Thanks." He hung up and looked at me. "Roma never made it to Chicago."

"What?"

"John called last night after the plane got in. She wasn't on it." Rich sat back and rubbed his face. "He had the airline check. She never made the flight. I called the Trolonski's. They saw her off in her rental. They also called the cops, but there's nothing they can do until twenty-four hours has elapsed. The Portland police are looking into it quietly but until that time..."

I shook my head in disbelief.

We sat in silence for several minutes. Finally Rich broke it. "Did you get the employee checks done yesterday?"

"All except two. I should have them done in about an hour." I looked at Rich, who was lost in thought. "Has Devon showed up anywhere?"

Rich's eyes met mine.

I didn't need the answer. I stood. "I'll be working on the checks."

Three hours later the phone rang interrupting my work. I listened as Pam told Rich that the call was for him. For some reason my heart was in my throat. Instinct told me this was not a good phone call.

I walked across the hall to Rich's office. He was already on the phone. He nodded as he listened. Then he closed his eyes. I swallowed and waited.

Rich nodded some more. "Thanks, Detective Yardley. I'll send all of our stuff out to you... Yes, I will... You'll be the first to get a call. Yes, Tom Hawkings. Thanks again." Rich slowly hung up the phone.

I sat down and waited.

Rich's eyes met mine.

"Roma?"

"The Oregon State Police found the car."

"And?"

"They found Roma too. Dead."

I cursed softly.

Rich nodded. "According to Detective Yardly it wasn't a pretty sight."

"Miles?"

"He hasn't shown up, but they got a ton of prints off of the car. They matched his. Roma fought hard and they will probably have DNA evidence to match up. When they find him."

I looked at my shoes, the tears started again. This was not a good week.

"Mel?"

I glanced up, Rich was staring at me.

"Are you okay?"

I shrugged. "First Earl. Now Roma." I took a deep breath and wiped at the tears. "How did Miles find her so fast?"

Rich grimaced. "I told her not to go to her parents. I knew it would be the first place he'd look, once he figured out we had tricked him. The best compromise I could work out with her was the two and a half day stay. I didn't want her to.... Maybe I should have insisted." He closed his eyes and ran both hands through his hair.

"Sounds like she chose, Rich. We can't be responsible for other people's choices."

"I know." Rich eyes remained closed. He leaned his head back. "Still, it doesn't make me feel any better."

"I talked to her Monday night. She was the happiest I had ever heard her. At least we gave her that."

"Yeah. At least that."

The silence drug out again. Neither of us moved. Pam's voice broke the quiet.

"John's on the phone, Rich."

Rich sat forward and opened his eyes as he picked up the phone. "Yeah?... No, head home. Roma was found by the Oregon State Police... Yeah... I know, John..." Rich looked at me. "I told her already... She's taking it pretty well." Rich smiled. "Sure... See you then."

"What'd John say?"

"When she wasn't on the plane, his first thought was that Devon found her. He tried to convince her not to go to her parents too, but she wouldn't listen to him either." Rich paused, then picked up his pen and paperwork. "He was worried how you were taking the news, after Boden and all."

"This had not been a good week."

Rich nodded. "That's for sure."

Pam poked her head in the door. "Delivery for Mel." She smiled as she handed me a small vase of flowers, then she left.

This bouquet was orchids in a crystal vase. I quickly found the note attached to the flowers as I sat the vase on Rich's desk. A warm feeling washing over me.

"Who are they from?"

"Max. I talked with him last night about Boden. We spoke at length. He, uh, talked me through the hard parts, now this."

Rich gave me a big brotherly smile.

I carried my bouquet back to my office. Although I felt bad about Boden and Roma, I knew that there was still good in the world. I carefully placed the flowers on the corner of the table and sat down.

The longer I sat and stared at the flowers the warmer I felt. I reached for the phone and dialed Max's number. His cell went to the answering service so I left a message. "Thanks for the flowers. Such a nice smelling hug."

I tried working, but my mind was muddled. So I sat looking at the flowers. They made me feel that there was life around me.

After a long time, Rich appeared at my doorway.

I looked at him.

"I know everyone keeps asking you this same question but, are you okay?"

I nodded. I saw Rich holding his hand behind his back. "What?"

Rich gave me his wry, big brother grin again. "I got another job for you."

I grimaced. If he was getting this big of a kick out of it, it had to be either gross or boring. "Yeah?"

Rich brought his hand from behind his back. It was a small garbage bag. He held it out to me.

"Oh no. I'm not going through any more grungy garbage. No way, Rich. I refuse. Fire me. I don't care. Once a month is too much for me."

"It's not garbage like you think. It's shredded papers." His grin got bigger. "I need them reassembled."

"Why me?"

Rich shrugged. "You used to like jigsaw puzzles."

"I hated jigsaw puzzles."

He chuckled. "Really?" He feigned innocence. "I thought you liked them."

"Give." I reached for the bag. "But you owe me."

"Put it on my bill," Rich said walking away.

Grumbling, I cleared my 'desk' of stuff. Opening up the bag, I huge pile of shavings landed with a plop. As I started sorting the little slips of papers, I mumbled nasty things about Rich, but they were only half-hearted nasty things. With a glance at the orchids and a deep satisfying sigh, I settled into piecing the papers back together.

Thanks

I want to thank all of my fans for hanging with me and waiting out the arrival of this book. So here it is and it's for you.

I also want to thank my critique partners and beta readers for all of their hard work. Cheryl, Ruth, Ray and Blane you guys are awesome. And don't forget to keep a special look out for something just for the four of you that I wrote into this book. Can you find it?

And as always, thanks to my biggest fans- my family. Without all of your love and support, I have no idea where I would be right now.

This book is dedicated to Scruffy. The real Scruffy. Rest in peace, little guy. I will never be able to forget my good friend's little toy poodle.